NIGHTWALKER 7

NIGHTWALKER 7

WRITTEN BY CRAIG MARTELLE, CREATED BY

FRANK RODERUS

DISRUPTIVE IMAGINATION

NIGHTWALKER 7 TEAM

Thanks to our Beta Readers

Micky Cocker, Dr. Jim Caplan, Kelly O'Donnell, and John
Ashmore

Thanks to our JIT Readers
John Ashmore
Kelly O'Donnell
Diane L. Smith
Deb Mader
Misty Roa
Peter Manis
Dorothy Lloyd
Jeff Goode
Micky Cocker

Editor
Lynne Stiegler

CHAPTER ONE

"I will have it fixed in just a minute, Miss Jennifer." Jim Wolfe turned the bicycle upside-down to put the front wheel in front of his face. He wore welding goggles because it was the daytime. The sun shone brightly and pained him mightily. His eyes were too sensitive to light but perfect for the night. He was the Nightwalker, a man who had survived the nuclear bombs by hiding underground for two years, existing on protein bars he had been carrying in his long-haul truck.

He waited until enough of the radiation had been absorbed by the forgiving earth.

When he emerged, his hair was white, and his beard no longer grew. He couldn't see in the daylight; the sun was blinding. His strength was beyond what a human should be capable of, and he could sense the tingle of radioactivity through his fingertips. During his time underground, the earth had made him into the perfect survivor, giving him the tools he needed to make the journey back home to Bradenton, Florida, where he had last seen Lurleen and little JoJo. That had been four years ago. JoJo would be six now.

Wolfe wondered if he would know him if he saw him. He would always remember his Lurleen, her blonde hair framing a glowing face. Would they recognize him? As his hair grew out, the dye job he had done was being replaced by white roots. Pretty soon, the brown would be gone, and he would once again stand out in a crowd.

Not that he, Jennifer, and Buddy, the big wolf/German Shepherd mix, ran across many crowds. They had made it to Laurel in what used to be Mississippi, taking back roads to head toward Mobile. From there, it was not far to Florida. He would finally get his answers.

If they could keep their bicycles going. The patch kit contained enough for at most two more repairs, depending on the damage to the tire. The bikes had been a gift from Abraham and the Faithful. Wolfe, Jennifer, and Buddy had covered more ground in the past three days than would have been possible any other way. Even the truck would not have been able to wend its way through the jumble of wreckage that littered the southern roadways.

In the aftermath of a war no one had known was coming, people had been in a hurry to go both ways, not knowing where they would find safety. All had suffered the same fate.

"It will be okay," Jennifer told him as if reading his mind. She kept her hand twisted in Buddy's thick neck hair. The big dog panted under the heat and humidity while sitting and watching.

Wolfe turned the bike over and used the small hand pump to inflate the tire. After it came up, he tested it to make sure the patch was solid. He climbed on and rode the bike in a small circle before rechecking the tire.

He nodded once to Jennifer. She understood and climbed back aboard her bike. "Buddy is wasting away." She pointed to the curve from his chest through his waist and back to his hips.

Wolfe threw his head back and laughed. "Buddy is finally getting enough exercise. I think he may be a lazy dog at heart."

Jennifer rolled her bike close enough to give Wolfe a shove. "He is a good dog. You take that back!" She shoved him again while chuckling. Buddy's tongue lolled as he hopped around, unsure of what was going on.

Wolfe turned serious. "We will head south to the water, then continue along the coast until we can see if Bradenton is still there. I fear the worst, Miss Jennifer. There are not many people down here. I think too many of the bombs landed on the military bases. The shipyards were probably targeted, too."

As they had traveled, he had opened up to his adopted daughter, sharing things you only share with family.

"It will be okay, Mister Wolfe. Are we close?"

"Maybe one hundred more miles, and we will be in Florida."

"By tonight?"

Wolfe shook his head. "Maybe by tomorrow night, if we do not run into any trouble."

"Trouble does not want to run into us," Jennifer replied. She slipped the tube from behind her shoulder and held it out. "I can shoot the eye out of a hummingbird at twenty paces."

Jim raised one eyebrow. "Bragging is not something we do, Miss Jennifer."

"I'm sorry." She hung her head for a moment before putting her makeshift blowgun away.

"But you have become a good shot in a very short time. Against men, we need something with a little more bite." He patted the butt of his AR-15. "I do not know why men had to turn into animals following a little thing like the end of civilization. Life goes on. All you have to do is keep your head."

The wreckage around them told the tale. A sign on the side of the road indicated they were on Highway 84. Wolfe removed his map from the waterproof pouch, carefully opening it to the right page. "Highway 84 to 45 and then south to Mobile."

He put his map away and sat there, hesitant to pedal forward.

"You need to know," Jennifer told him. "I will be with you, no matter the truth."

Wolfe brightened briefly before the dark cloud returned. "I know you will, Miss Jennifer. The closer we get, the harder it is to put one foot in front of the other."

Jennifer smiled and waved. "Just like this." She made a tight turn to face the bike east and pedaled casually off.

"Maybe it *is* as easy as that." He followed quickly, not wanting to let her get too far away. The wild pressed in on the road—trees, shrubs, and broken vehicles. Too many places for men like the wilders to hide. He hurried ahead until they rode side by side. When debris cluttered their path, Wolfe rode first, slowly picking his way through.

Another mile, and another after that. They continued through the day without flat tires or meeting another human being. They saw small deer in the distance, but not close enough to get a shot. Buddy loped after them, indifferent to running

Wolfe was worried that Florida would be a wasteland.

As they turned south toward the Gulf coast, he felt the strange tingle of radiation coming from the nearby town. The sign said it was Waynesboro. The feeling put him on edge.

CHAPTER TWO

"Don't touch anything," Wolfe warned. They continued for another mile before Wolfe held up his hand to stop.

The big dog headed for a puddle by the side of the road. Wolfe grabbed him before he drank.

"We need to turn back," Wolfe said in a low voice. "This area is hot with radiation. We will get you a drink where it is safe." Wolfe looked the dog in the face before scratching his ear and pushing him away from the water.

Jennifer called the dog as she turned around without question and headed away from the red zone. With one last glance over his shoulder, Wolfe followed her.

Wolfe stopped them when they reached a side road that led south. He checked his map, to find that a great number of small roads crisscrossed the area. He put out the kickstand on his bike and checked the water in a small stream that flowed nearby, relaxing and taking a drink before calling Buddy and Jennifer over.

He watched while they drank. When they finished, he spoke. "Hide the bicycles, and we will stay here for the night."

Wolfe never took his eyes from a small stand of woods nearby. He held his finger to his lips and stalked off ninety degrees to his target before turning and heading in. Buddy wanted to follow. The big dog sensed a hunt, but Jennifer held him back. When he sat down, she released her hold and pulled out her blowgun. The longer she sat unmoving, the more birds flew into the area.

She loaded a small ball bearing taken from a wrecked vehicle and slowly raised the tube, then waited for a blue jay to stop hopping around on a wire overhead. With a quick exhale, she sent the bearing straight and true, hitting the bird under its chin. Stunned, it dropped within two paces of her. She waited, hoping it would not recover its senses before she had two or three more in hand.

As she lined up on the second jay, a shot rang out, scaring the birds off the line. Jennifer checked the woods but could see nothing. An animal growled, low and rising to a terrible scream. Tree branches broke, and the ground trembled under the distant fury of a great beast. Wolfe fired again and again.

Jennifer walked carefully to the blue jay on the ground, grabbed it quickly by the head, and spun it. She hurried back to Buddy and crouched beside him. The dog vibrated as Wolfe's AR-15 barked repeatedly.

Jennifer hugged the big dog. What was Wolfe shooting at? What if someone else was shooting at him? Her thoughts traced a chaotic path through her mind as she looked around. They were in the middle of nowhere, the heat and humidity pressing in on her along with a growing cloud of flies and bugs. She waved the blue jay around her head to drive them away.

Buddy took an interest in the bird, watching it intensely. With the last shot long behind, the big dog was no longer concerned about the woods. Jennifer tried to see into the shadows beyond the trees. Silence returned—complete silence, not a bird or the wind. Soon the sound of buzzing insects reached her ears.

The girl hesitated as Wolfe emerged from the shadows of the trees and waved at her. She breathed a sigh of relief, relaxing enough that Buddy got the opportunity he was waiting for. He yanked the bird from her hand and bolted down the weed-infested road.

Jennifer jumped up and took two steps, but the dog was already happily munching his prize. She scanned the sky, but the birds had gone. Wolfe motioned for her to join him.

Jennifer took one look at the bikes and decided to move them into the ditch before heading into the woods.

Wolfe waited patiently. They had to be vigilant. He had not been when he'd first entered the new world after the bombs fell, and he'd paid for it by running afoul of the wilders, and especially the Alston brothers. Knowing what he knew now, he would have opted for killing them outright instead of letting any of them go, but he did not know that then. Wolfe did not consider himself a killer. He only wanted to get home and find out if Lurleen and JoJo were alive.

He was training the girl to be more aware. She was learning her lessons well.

When Jennifer and Buddy joined Wolfe, he pointed at a dark spot nearby. A large black bear had plowed a furrow in the soft earth of the forest floor where it had slid to a stop, dying mid-charge. Wolfe already had his knife in hand.

"Are you hungry?" he asked with a smile. Buddy raced to it, barking and nipping at the dead bear while Jennifer nodded.

CHAPTER THREE

Three days later, they had as much smoked bear meat as they could carry. Since they were omnivores with a diet rich in berries, fruits, and vegetables, black bear meat made for good eating.

Wolfe, Jennifer, and especially Buddy had eaten well, and the smoke from the process had held off the insects, letting them get uninterrupted sleep. When it was time to get back on the road, they discovered two of the bike tires were flat. Wolfe looked at his patch kit and the damage.

"I will fix your tire," he told Jennifer. "But it looks like I have to walk." He had enough of the repair kit to fix both, but then he would have nothing left. Wolfe knew that he could maintain a running pace, letting the girl ride easily along. They could cover more ground than if both were walking. He pocketed the remaining patch material before blowing up Jennifer's tire.

They headed south. Wolfe kept the morning sun on his left shoulder, following his nose when it was time to turn east. They meandered through the countryside. Wolfe jogged while Jennifer followed him closely, riding smoothly. She had quickly become an expert, although she had never ridden before a couple of weeks prior. The big dog ran from ditch to ditch, tongue lolling as he tried to stay cool. His thick hair was not suited for the heat of a fast-approaching Southern summer.

Wolfe stopped for a short rest, adjusting his welding goggles and wiping off the outer lens for the thousandth time that day. The hazy gray that reached his eyes was further misted because of the scratches from wearing the goggles during the daylight hours every day since he had found them. They were reaching the end of their usability. He added the search for new goggles to the short list of things he had to do.

"Where did the people go?" Jennifer asked after taking a long drink from a canteen.

"I do not know, Miss Jennifer. Maybe they died from the radiation, but nothing shows that this area was hit. There is no atomic wasteland like we saw out west, and everything is growing like it should. Maybe the people went north. Without air conditioning, I cannot imagine who in their right mind would live down here." He chuckled. He had been one of those people but had always had indoor air conditioning as an escape from the heat, humidity, and bugs.

His smile faded. *No one in their right mind.*

Wolfe was pressing south—much farther south. What if Lurleen and JoJo had come north to escape the swamp and jungle of a pre-industrial-age Florida? He clenched his teeth. The more he thought about it, the less he realized he knew.

Jennifer pedaled out first as they reached a wide country road with few wrecks and light weeds making their way into the sun through the cracked pavement. In the distance, a four-lane overpass loomed. Wolfe ran in front and held Jennifer back. He opened his map to see where they were.

"Highway 45, and soon, we will cross the border into

what used to be Alabama." Wolfe pulled his glasses down and rubbed his eyes. When he was ready to go, he found Jennifer watching him.

He nodded briefly and started walking. She joined him without a word. They had said everything that needed to be said. Wolfe turned up the on-ramp and headed south toward Mobile.

Within minutes, he heard a pop and the grind of the rim on the concrete. Jennifer stopped and got off her bike, then flipped it upside down to make it easy for Wolf to fix the front tire. He dropped his pack and dug out the repair kit.

Jennifer took out her blowgun while she waited. Buddy barked and danced out of the way as a snake slithered from the thick grass on the side of the road. It moved sideways to them before turning and darting quickly toward Wolfe. Jennifer loosed a ball bearing. She hit the snake and knocked it off balance, but it recovered quickly.

"Watch out!" she called as it closed. Wolfe turned, and with inhuman speed, he lashed out and caught the snake behind its head. Its fangs were extended and ready to bury themselves in his calf. He squeezed and crushed the life from it. When it hung limp, he cast it away. Buddy attacked the dead snake, gripping it in his mouth, growling and shaking his head.

"I think he is supposed to do that *before* the snake is killed," Wolfe offered.

"He is a good dog," Jennifer replied, thrusting out her chest in defiance. Buddy kept up his antics until the snake split in half. Then he looked at it in confusion before returning to Jennifer with his tongue hanging out and his tail wagging.

Wolfe nodded, but something else held his attention. The bike's tire had split along one of the tube repair seams. He could not fix it. The tubes from his tires were too big, so he had not bothered bringing the one that still held air.

"Looks like we are walking from here," Wolfe said.

Jennifer shrugged. She slipped her backpack on, checked the bike to see if there was anything she needed from it, and without complaint, started walking.

Wolfe shrugged on his pack, then checked his bow and few remaining arrows before deciding to carry the rifle in his hand. He slung the bow over his pack and jogged after Jennifer and the big dog.

CHAPTER FOUR

On the third day traveling 45 south, they finally saw another human. The person was grubbing along the shore, and when they saw Wolfe and the others, they made themselves scarce by disappearing into the brush.

Wolfe stopped and listened. Jennifer cocked her ears as well. "I hear him running away."

"I guess they are not used to strangers appearing from the north. I wonder what happened that they are afraid of?" Wolfe kept his rifle at the ready while they continued. At one point in time, Mobile's urban sprawl had reached this far north. Wolfe was not sure how far away they were, but he knew the interstate that led east ran through the center of town. "We have a ways to go. Ten miles, maybe."

Jennifer did not show any concern about the distance. Maybe it did not mean anything to her.

"Four hours of walking," Wolfe added.

Her eyes brightened. "Not far at all." The big dog strolled slowly along, watching the ditches from under bowed brows.

"Next stream, we better stop to let Buddy get a drink."

"It is too hot for him." Jennifer ruffled his ears, and the dog perked up. "Is it always this hot where you used to live?"

"Pretty much." Wolfe kept it simple. They would get used to it over time.

Another mile and more people, this time less fearful and more curious. Two men and a woman walked into the roadway and waited for them. Jennifer tightened her grip on the big dog. Wolfe waved and stopped when they were still ten yards away. He aimed the barrel of his rifle toward the ground, but he had his hand on the pistol-grip and finger outside the trigger housing. The magazine was inserted with a round in the chamber. Wolfe had been ambushed too many times to take unnecessary risks.

Jennifer peeked out from behind him.

"Howdy, stranger," one of the men called, waving a hand in greeting.

Wolfe nodded. He was not one for volunteering information.

"Where are you coming from?" the woman asked when the silence became uncomfortable.

"All the way from Idaho. Most recently from Little Rock."

The three started talking among themselves, keeping their voices low, but they waved their arms and pointed while shifting their feet nervously. Finally, the woman stepped away from the trio.

"We have heard that there is nothing up there. It is all a wasteland, populated by the desperate and dying, preyed on by mutant wild animals."

Wolfe wiped his forehead with the back of his arm and shook his head slowly. "The world is healing itself. There are very few hot spots. The greenery you see here is what you'll see for a hundred miles north and west. The wildlife is recovering, and a sharp hunter will find plenty to eat. Have you ever had smoked black bear?"

One of the men nodded. "A long time ago, mister. We do not have rifles like you. Well, we do, but no ammunition. That is long spent."

"On what?" Wolfe asked. *If they did not hunt, what were they shooting?*

The trio shuffled nervously. "Wasted on nothing good," the woman finally admitted. "My name is Maribelle. This here is Chase, and he's Hiram." The two men nodded when their names were spoken.

"Jim Wolfe. My daughter Jennifer, and that there is Buddy." Wolfe stayed where he was. Introductions did not mean it was safe to pass. "We want to get to Florida, Bradenton, south of Tampa. My wife and son were there before the bombs fell." Wolfe finally took his eyes off the trio and looked at the ground. "It has taken us this long to get here. I hope we will be able to pass without any problems."

Maribelle cast a look at Chase on her right and then at Hiram on her left. She grimaced. "I do not know how to tell you this, but there ain't nothing left of that part of Florida. Big military base over there got the worst of it. Bases along the Panhandle, too. The enemy hit fast and furious. We were spared here in Mobile, but no one knows why. Maybe they ran out of bombs before we were important enough to destroy. Hell, no one knows why the war started."

Jennifer gripped Wolfe's arm to give him what support she could.

"You thought there was nothing to the north, but that information was not correct. If you do not mind, I will see for myself."

"Of course." The woman shrugged. "There are a lot of people in the city. It might be best to hide that gun of yours. If you only want to pass through, best not to stand out."

"That is mighty kind of you." Wolfe stood his ground. The three locals waved and left the road, clearing the way ahead.

After Wolfe and Jennifer started walking again, they looked for a place to hide. He led them into a small area without any sounds of life. Broken-down homes with weeds overgrowing them were all around. He forced his way into one, covering the entrance behind them. "I will take a look tonight. Keep your head down and stay quiet, and you and Buddy will be safe."

They ate cold smoked bear—not the most tender of meals, but better than much they had eaten over the past year.

Once finished, Wolfe reclined against the wall and quickly fell asleep.

CHAPTER FIVE

It was well after midnight, Wolfe sat on a small hill watching a city that did not sleep. As many people were out and about at night as had been during the daytime. It was much cooler now without the merciless sun beating down.

The people in Mobile had developed a system of gas lighting along many of the main streets. They were not that bright, but they chased away the darkness and limited Wolfe's advantage. He was able to see without his goggles by squinting to keep out the faint light that struck him. The Gulf lapped peacefully in the near distance. Built on a river's delta like New Orleans not far away, the blast from the nuclear weapons or the cataclysm that was the planet's surface's reply to the violence done to it, the bay had entered the city, submerging the part closest to the shoreline.

Wolfe looked for a path to get closer, see what the action was about, learn what he needed to know to get through the city without running afoul of the locals. He worked his way through the back alleys, sticking to the shadows. A series of warehouse-type structures had the majority of the activity, the most people coming and going. Wolfe kept his welding goggles off and squinted to block out the hazy gas lights.

He found himself between the building and the Gulf waters that lapped a rough-built dock. He dodged into the darkness, finding himself hip-deep in runoff from the building. The smell of rotting fish threatened to overwhelm him. Wolfe covered his face with a sleeve, trying to ignore the fish slime as a steam-powered ship slowly lumbered in. The small vessel activated its spotlights to help it maneuver in the tight spaces.

Wolfe gasped in pain, clenching his eyes shut and frantically pulling his goggles down. When he could open his eyes again, he found the ship's efforts were focused on getting to the dock and not on finding people lurking in the shadows. A small group of men and women from the warehouse pushed carts to the newly arrived vessel. With the help of a small steam-powered crane onboard the vessel, the ship's few crew loaded the carts with fish. The leader of the warehouse group, the only one not grunting with the effort of moving the catch, gave the ship's captain a small slip of paper. The two shook hands before the captain jumped easily from the dock to the casually bobbing ship's deck. With a short command, the ship undocked and headed back out into the darkness of the Gulf.

The shore party pushed their carts back into the warehouse, and darkness returned.

Wolfe climbed out of the fish waste runoff and ran through the shadows to get away from the heart of the bay.

Numerous streams cut through the city. He dove into the first one that looked remotely clean. He scrubbed hard at his clothes and his body, soaking in the cool water as he tried to get the stench out.

When he emerged, the city had finally slowed. He figured it was about three in the morning. A causeway led to the east past the USS *Alabama* memorial. The big ship floated serenely, outlined against the darkened sky. Wolfe didn't want to get trapped on the causeway, so he let it go. When they traveled it, they would be heading out of the city on their way to Florida. His destination was close.

The humidity and smell of the ocean mixed with the stink of rotted fish reminded him of home. Odd. He had never thought of the fish smell until it was on him, and then he could think of nothing else.

His mind worked, reviewing the things he had seen while hiding in the fish slop. The workers from the warehouse had been happy, joking as they loaded their carts. The ship's crew was, too. The two men had shaken hands in a friendly way.

He listened carefully, hearing the sounds of song and play. Wolfe worked his way closer to a building that looked like a bar. He listened by an open side window. People were enjoying themselves. With his goggles in place, he risked a look and saw a variety of faces—men and women, laughing and drinking, but not drunk.

"One more for the road?" an older man asked.

"Everyone's had their limit. You know the rules. Until we have a bumper crop, everyone gets an equal shot at two drinks."

"I guess we better get out there and make sure we bring home the wheat!" The crowd erupted in laughter.

Wolfe did not understand what they were talking about, but the feeling was different from the other places he had been. The revelers accepted the limitation with shrugs and good humor, waving as they rose and headed out. Wolfe disappeared into the shadows once more, selecting a young couple to follow home.

He pulled his goggles down to follow the couple, who walked with the confidence of familiarity. They had walked that road a thousand times and could do it with their eyes closed. The gas lights were few and far between, but the couple never wavered. Wolfe stayed off the road in case they looked back, but they walked without worry.

Wolfe stepped on a stick and it broke. When he jumped to the side, he landed in a pile of gravel that slid and rolled. The couple turned around easily and walked straight to him. He stood up straight as if he meant to be there.

"Slipped in the darkness," he told them.

"Where are you headed, mister?" the young woman asked.

"Where we are staying. Up that way." He waved in a general direction away from where Jennifer and Buddy were hidden. "I do not have any local currency, but I could smell the beer back there. What would it take to get one?"

"You must be new," the young man replied, his facial expression not changing. "Scrip. We get paid in notes, and those are used for trade. It works pretty well. All you need is a job, and there is plenty of work to be had. More than we can do."

"Who is in charge down here? It does not sound like FEDCOM."

"FEDCOM? I do not know what that is, mister, but here in Mobile, the old council runs things. I got no complaints." The man nodded to the woman. She agreed.

"Maybe we will stick around for a spell. I could use a few regular meals." Wolfe had plenty of smoked bear in the house with Jennifer, but he did not want to give up the meat, as he had done outside Little Rock. He could not abide helping people who were out to hurt him.

"There is plenty for those willing and able to work. I cannot see you that well in the dark, but you sound healthy enough. Show up at the warehouse on Beauregard tomorrow morning. Well, I guess that would be later this morning. Ask for Keaton. He will show you what is available," the man explained.

"I think I will do just that. I thank you kindly." Wolfe waved but expected the couple could not see the gesture. He backed away and disappeared into the darkness. The couple said goodbye to the space where Wolfe had been before continuing on their way.

CHAPTER SIX

When Jennifer and Buddy woke up, Wolfe was there, leaning against the wall as he had been before they fell asleep.

"Did you go out?" the girl asked.

Wolfe nodded, still replaying the events of the night before. Jennifer held her nose and pointed at him.

"There was an unfortunate meeting of my body and the spirit of the fish that are feeding the city."

Jennifer cocked her head. Buddy shied away and departed out the front door to do his business.

"Are you going to wash?" Jennifer asked innocently enough. "I guess I could get used to it, but I am not sure anyone else will."

Wolfe thought about her innocence and hung his head. They could keep going, rotting as they walked, or they could stay for a while. Get a job and live like normal people. The words from the locals stabbed into his soul. Bradenton was not there? He found it easy to believe and the speakers believable. They had nothing to gain by lying.

"We need to sort things out, so what do you say we stay

here for a while? I think I can find work that pays. It does not look like anyone will be getting into our business. The people 'round here are good Southern folk, kind and welcoming. Southern hospitality, they used to call it. I wonder if they have grits?"

"What about Florida?" Jennifer purposely did not mention Lurleen and JoJo.

"If it is still there, it will be there a little while longer. I need a bath, and you need some proper schooling."

Jennifer stood up and jammed her fists on her hips. She was going to argue, but the look on Wolfe's face suggested her words would fall on deaf ears. Buddy returned, happy as could be with a squirrel in his mouth. He laid in the corner, using his powerful jaws to tear his breakfast apart, chewing happily.

"As long as they will let me bring Buddy." She stood her ground.

"Southern hospitality," Wolfe repeated. "Get your stuff. As soon as the dog is finished, we will head into town, find us a proper place to stay, and maybe get a bath."

"Maybe?" Jennifer wondered.

Wolfe grinned broadly. He did not like it when he could smell himself. If he could not get his clothes clean, he would be willing to burn them. The smell seemed to grow over time despite having rinsed once already.

"Probably," he conceded.

Jennifer wrestled with the big dog to keep him from gagging on the bushy tail. After the battle ended with the young girl waving the tail over her head, Wolfe gestured toward the door. He put on his pack, within which he had hidden the rifle. He carried his bow in his right hand, using it to push the greenery out of the way to leave the house. He held the bushes back so Jennifer could walk out without having to fight her way through. Buddy bounded after her.

Wolfe had held the brush out of the way for the dog, too. There had been a time when Wolfe had not bothered to give the dog a name. He had come and gone as he pleased and fended for himself, but the two were inseparable, thanks to the Alstons. A common enemy had bound them. And with Jennifer, a common friend now served the same purpose.

"Where are we going, Mister Wolfe?" Jennifer asked.

"Where we can get the answers to our questions," Wolfe replied cryptically. He frowned as he walked. Miles to go before Beauregard Street. He hoped the warehouse would be obvious and Mister Keaton would stand out from the crowd.

Until then, he needed to gather his thoughts.

The three walked in silence past a growing number of people, who waved and smiled.

CHAPTER SEVEN

The warehouse was obvious. It smelled just like Jim Wolfe. More fish processing.

Wolfe wondered if they did anything else this close to the bay. Jennifer held her nose and looked knowingly at him.

"Stay here. I will be back as soon as I can."

Jennifer nodded and took hold of Buddy's neck fur. The big dog panted heavily but sat down on the warm pavement and watched as Wolfe walked toward the warehouse's open double doors that stood above an unused loading dock.

At one time, trucks would have backed up to that dock and been loaded by forklifts working in square dance-like precision. There were no trucks that Wolfe could see or hear, even though the town had a central gas system for its lighting. He wondered what else they used their resource for.

At the doors to the warehouse-turned-fish-processing-facility, a man with a clipboard watched and counted. "I am looking for a man called Keaton."

"It is your lucky day!" the man replied, clapping Wolfe on the shoulder. "You found him. Sent here for work?"

"I was." Wolfe took the full measure of the man. Average

height, average build, maybe a little thin, but he was ready with a genuine smile and a sparkle in his eyes.

"You good at cutting fish? We're in the middle of a quick freeze, so we have a little time to train you if need be."

"My daddy taught me right. I can clean and fillet anything that swims."

"Great!" Keaton exclaimed, gesturing with his head toward the end of a long table where four women stood an arms' length apart, working a slow-moving conveyor belt. "You can start right now, Mister…ah, I didn't get your name."

"Wolfe. Jim Wolfe. And that there is my daughter Jennifer and her dog Buddy." Wolfe pointed at the pair across the parking lot. "I'd like to get her into a proper school. I'm more than willing to work as hard as it takes to provide for us."

Keaton looked Wolfe up and down. "You look like you have worked hard already." Jennifer waved. "And done right by them. I tell you what. I'll hire her for today only, cleaning up, and after your shift is over, I'll introduce you to Mister Graves, the schoolmaster. Everyone who works on the bay sends their kids right there," he pointed at a building across the road, "to make it easy to drop them off and pick them up."

"Just like the world used to be," Wolfe said softly.

"People work. They support their families. They enjoy their lives," Keaton said. "We had no control over what happened to the world, but we can control how we respond to it. We are doing our best to keep on keeping on."

Wolfe nodded and waved for Jennifer to join them. When she arrived, she curtsied to the foreman.

"I see you were taught good manners." Keaton smiled down at Jennifer. "You already fit in just fine. Let me show you what I need you to do."

The foreman didn't question Buddy's presence, leaving

the big dog to keep Jennifer company as she scrubbed the floor under and around the conveyor.

Buddy leaned over the conveyor and grabbed a cleaned fish that was headed for the freezer room. Wolfe groaned and hurried to Jennifer. "You have to keep Buddy away from the fish. He is going to cost us our paychecks," Wolfe warned.

Jennifer agreed while staring at the floor. She found a piece of rope and tied it around his big neck and looped the other end around her waist. When she got back to work, she found herself in a constant tug-of-war with Buddy. He had become fascinated by the fish, especially since he was always hungry. Jennifer had to finally give up. She found the foreman and extended her apologies.

"I am sorry. You gave me a chance, but I will not be able to continue. Buddy is trying to take fish off the conveyor. You keep what I earned so far to pay for the one fish he managed to get." She turned to catch Wolfe's eye. "I'll be outside whenever you finish, Mister Wolfe."

He nodded to her without missing a beat with his filleting knife. He ran it across the strop and kept moving. Soon, he was sharing tips with the other workers. They talked back and forth until they worked their way through the three cartloads that had been waiting and two more that arrived while they were there.

When they finished, Keaton strolled to the back dock and shielded his eyes as he scanned the harbor. "Nothing new coming in. Looks like we're done early today. Good job, people."

He walked back into the warehouse. The cutting crew surrounded the foreman. Wolfe followed them over and stood on the outside looking in. The foreman handed strips of paper to each worker.

Scrip. He handed a full pack to each, pulling two from Wolfe's pack because he joined the team later in the morning and hadn't worked a full shift. Keaton looked at the two scrip after the others had walked away. He shoved them into Wolfe's hand. "For the girl's work. One fish is all your dog ate? That is on the house. Take a couple for your dinner, and we'll see you tomorrow morning 'round seven."

Keaton pointed to the schoolhouse before adding, "You might want to bring clothes you do not mind getting the fish smell on and change here. We got lockers in the back."

"I want to thank you for your help. There are not many people left in this world like you," Wolfe said slowly.

"You earned your keep, Jim." The foreman gave him a little push toward the door. "Go on now. We will see you in the A.M."

Wolfe headed outside to find Jennifer and Buddy resting in the shade. They perked up when they saw him. Wolfe pointed toward the school, and they intercepted him on his way. "School is right there. Mister Graves will see that you get proper schooling while we are here."

Jennifer clenched her jaw and chose to stay silent.

He noted her response. He was not sure what it meant, but he did not challenge her. They made the walk quickly and in silence. Inside the building, there were numerous rooms. It looked like it had been a school before the bombs, with individual desks. Maybe it had been a church, and these were the Sunday school classrooms.

There was a smattering of students throughout, together by size, which generally meant by age and ability. All eyes turned to the strangers walking through the hall. Wolfe and Jennifer both noticed it. There were no other pets. Probably a good thing, so Buddy did not start a fight. He had not been around other dogs.

Wolfe stopped when he realized that he had not seen an adult in any of the rooms. He stuck his head into the classroom with the oldest kids. "I beg your pardon. We are looking for Mister Graves."

One boy pointed down the hallway. Wolfe nodded politely. They had already been that way. They retraced their steps but leaned inside each room to check before continuing. In the back of one, they found him—a diminutive adult sitting at a small desk next to a child, talking softly with her. They waited for him to notice them. When he did, he rose and came to them, motioning for them to move into the hallway.

"Can I help you?" His eyes kept darting to the dog.

"This is Jennifer, Jennifer Wolfe. We just arrived and will be here for a while. I want to get my daughter some proper schooling until we move on."

"Of course. What grade is she in?"

Wolfe stared back without answering. Jennifer stepped up. "I have never been to a school, but I can read."

The schoolmaster didn't have far to lean down to look Jennifer in the eye. "How old are you? Twelve? Thirteen?"

"Thirteen," she answered. "I'll be fourteen soon."

"I am glad that you can read. That is the minimum standard for a nearly fourteen-year-old, but better than some we have gotten. School opens at seven and closes at seven, but we have daycare until ten if you work one of the fishing boats." He looked pointedly at Wolfe's disheveled appearance, his nose twitching at the smell.

"Miss Jennifer will be cleaned up when we come back tomorrow, as will I," Wolfe assured him.

Buddy barked to get everyone's attention after having been left out of the conversation for too long.

"And Buddy will be with her," Wolfe stated in a way that did not allow for rejection. The schoolmaster tried to stare him down, but the welding goggles got in his way.

"Why do you wear those?"

"My eyes are a little sensitive to light. Do you know if there is a welding shop around here? I could use a new pair."

The man nodded and led them to the door. He pointed at the warehouse where Wolfe had spent the day working. Wolfe could not tell if the man was trying to pull one over on them or not.

"I will see you tomorrow," Mister Graves told Jennifer before conceding to Jim Wolfe's iron will. "Both of you."

He patted Buddy's head and returned to his classrooms.

Jennifer held her nose.

"So, we have two things to do," Wolfe said, gesturing with his head toward the warehouse while looking at his jeans, bothered that he had gotten used to the smell. They left the school and returned to the fish-processing building.

Keaton looked surprised when Wolfe, Jennifer, and Buddy walked back in.

Wolfe held up his hands so he would not alarm the foreman. "I have a couple questions. Do you do any welding in here?"

"Used to. Ran out of oxygen, so we are hard down."

"Do you have any extra goggles? My eyes are sensitive to light, and sunglasses are not dark enough." Wolfe felt less restrained in sharing his limitation, although he did not bother telling them that he could see at night as if it were daytime.

"Let's see," Keaton offered and waved for them to follow. Buddy sniffed at the conveyor as they passed. "You said you had two questions."

"Do you know any place nearby where we might be able to stay?"

"Sure. There's a loft upstairs, but people do not stay long because of the smell."

Jennifer giggled.

"You are welcome to it. One scrip a night, comes with

towels and running water."

"We'll take it!" Jennifer said before Wolfe could reply.

They walked through a metal door and into a darkened room. "Sorry. No lights in here," Keaton apologized. Jennifer took him by the hand and left Wolfe on his own, shutting the door behind them.

"He will be just fine. Give him a minute," she explained. The foreman asked about the dog and how far they had traveled. Jennifer talked about Buddy but did not have to answer the rest because Wolfe opened the door.

"I would be much obliged to buy these from you," Wolfe said, holding up a pair of goggles that looked like the ones he had on and a second set that looked more like a ski mask.

"Take 'em," Keaton waved the goggles away as if brushing off a fly. Wolfe thrust four scrip into the foreman's hand.

"For the room and your kindness." Wolfe refused to take any back.

"As you wish. It will be nice to have someone up there. It gives the place a more homey feel, and we all could use a little more of that."

Wolfe nodded, and with Jennifer and Buddy, they headed up a staircase on the side of the fish-processing floor to find two doors along a small hallway. One held a room with two twin beds and the other a bathroom with a tub. Two towels were folded neatly on the sink, and a bar of lye soap was next to the tub. Wolfe dumped his pack and gear in the room.

Jennifer stood with her arms crossed.

"Hey!" she remarked when he made to sit down on the bed. She pointed with her arm outstretched toward the bathroom. Wolfe smiled as he held his hands up in surrender. Just to be sure, he closed the door at the top of the steps. He dug in his pack for his rifle, putting it together to use as a brace against the doorknob. He smiled at Jennifer and disappeared into the bathroom. She watched the rifle as if it would move, sighing heavily that they still felt they had to take such precautions.

Four scrip sat on Wolfe's bed. She took it and started to leave to go buy food, but she thought better of it, putting it back and sitting on her bed with Buddy to wait for Wolfe to finish. She wondered what kind of routine they would settle into. It had been a while since they'd stayed in any one place for longer than a day or two.

Jim's pants were soaked, but after a liberal application of the lye soap, they no longer smelled, and neither did he. Jennifer took only ten minutes, vowing to wash her clothes before they went to bed.

Wolfe grimaced with each step in his wet clothes, but the heat suggested he would dry quickly, while simultaneously sweating. A small vent was on the floor. Wolfe flipped it with his toe and cold air poured out.

"We are over the freezer," Wolfe said, wondering why the exhaust wasn't hot, but this was something an ingenious tenant must have installed, tapping into the cooler. Buddy dove in first, biting at the cool air until he laid in front of it with his nose over the vent. "Are you hungry?"

Jennifer nodded but did not smile when he reached for his pack. He stopped.

"Let us see if we can find a place to eat." With four scrip in hand, they headed out, dragging the big dog away from the cool air but leaving the vent open and closing the door. They looked forward to returning to the cool room for a good night's rest.

Wolfe took Jennifer to the small bar that he had lingered outside of the night prior. It smelled the same but different from the night before. The young couple was there, and they recognized him.

"Mister! Welcome back." They both sniffed before giving him a thumbs-up.

After the introductions, the young couple called for the bartender to serve up bowls of the daily catch.

In less than a minute, two oversized bowls filled with rich and thick fish stew appeared. It had more fish and vegetables than broth. Buddy looked put out, but Wolfe had brought a few slices of bear jerky to keep him occupied while they ate.

The young couple watched the exchange, eyes fixed on the red meat. Wolf tore off two small pieces and handed them over. "Much obliged for your help yesterday," he said.

After one bite and a long slow savoring chew, the young man smiled and turned to the bartender. "Get this man a beer!"

CHAPTER EIGHT

A week later, Miss Jennifer had a boyfriend. Wolfe had not expected anything like that, and it caught him off-guard. He wondered if facing the Alstons had been easier on his soul.

Wolfe worked hard during the day, and Jennifer studied hard in school with Buddy by her side. Wolfe wondered if Buddy was learning anything, but he had more pressing matters to think about—like what to do about the fifteen-year-old from Mobile.

"Why do you have to do anything?" Jennifer asked as the two relaxed in their room, the vent taking the edge off the summer heat.

"I do not think it is time for a relationship. We will be moving on soon. We have to."

Jennifer hung her head and started to cry. She needed the stability of their lives here. He needed to find out what happened to his wife and son. He had vowed to protect her and could not do that if she stayed behind.

"I am going to take a job on one of the fishing boats to make more scrip and set us up a little better."

Jennifer snuffled and nodded.

Fourteen was too young but old enough. Wolfe had wanted her to be able to stand on her own, but now that she was stepping out, he was lost. He felt like he needed to do something. "What do you want me to do?" he deferred.

"Like him?"

"I will try," was the best he could commit to. As night fell, darkening the single heavily clouded window, Wolfe tried to sleep, but his troubled thoughts held his rest at bay.

Wolfe had enough scrip from a week in the fish-processing warehouse to pay the rent now that he wasn't working there, but Keaton had recommended that Wolfe join a fishing boat to maybe increase the amount of fish caught. Keaton had been kind enough to offer to rent him the place while there was a lull. He hoped Wolfe would return once the fishing picked up when the weather changed from the heat of summer.

The fishing boat was moored two docks down from the fish-processing warehouse. Wolfe was early by a long stretch. It was well before dawn, but that was when Jim Wolfe was the most comfortable. He strolled along the darkened wharf, a new one built after the bombs and flooding had filled the bay. Wolfe was not sure if the water had risen or the land had sunk. He did not waste time speculating about the past when the present occupied his mind, along with the future. Would they take the new boy with them, or would Jennifer stay here?

Wolfe did not have answers to those questions and suspected he would never have the right answer. The more pressing matter was making a good showing on the fishing boat. He was a lifelong fisherman but had never done it commercially. The process was different. Wolfe relaxed. No need to worry about fishing. The job would get done. He wanted to get on a bigger trawler, one that went all the way to Florida's mid-Gulf coast, and more specifically, Bradenton.

Not that he was tired of walking, but that would answer many questions in as short a time as possible. Then he could get back to dealing with Jennifer's boyfriend. He smirked. If that was the worst thing he had to worry about, life was pretty good. He pushed that out of his mind to focus on fishing and running the boat.

He pulled his new welding goggles over his eyes and enjoyed the clear vision he had through clean and unscratched lenses. And he waited.

The captain was the first to arrive. Wolfe met him on the dock, and the two shook hands. "I would have prepped the boat, but I do not know what to do. I will fix that tomorrow," Wolfe promised.

The captain nodded. "Early riser?" he asked, squinting to see in the darkness. "Let's light things up."

The captain lit a candle using an old Zippo lighter. He kindled the fire under the boiler after checking the water level and supply of firewood. Wolfe hadn't seen anyone moving those supplies.

"Do you know how to operate a boiler?" the captain asked.

"Yes, sir. We had a boiler for heat back when I was a boy. Where did you get the wood?"

The captain threw his head back and laughed. "We moor here because it's close to our homes, but we supply the boat across the bay. Wood and fresh water. We have enough to get over there, filling up in the morning. We trade wood and water for fish, so we don't run with too heavy a draft. We get better speed that way."

Wolfe took in the information. One other crewman arrived. He went by Rusty. Wolfe never caught the captain's name, but it was not his to learn. It was the captain's to share, and he seemed perfectly happy to go by "Captain." Many people had distanced themselves from their lives before the bombs fell.

For Wolfe, though, that would have meant abandoning Lurleen and JoJo. He embraced his past and his present. "I'm Jim Wolfe," he said loudly. "This rig ever sail close to the Tampa area?"

"Nah. We don't go out that far. We are a little small for that trip. We would have to carry too much firewood. The *Sallie Mae* goes out that far. She is a seventy-footer, a big ol' gal. Hey! Don't you tell me you are going to jump ship? What do you think is down that way?"

"My wife and son were down there when the bombs fell. I have to see for myself if they survived. I have been working these past four years to get back."

"Hell, mister, there ain't nothing left," Rusty said nonchalantly.

"If it will make you feel better, we can cruise by *Sallie* and ask her crew," the captain offered.

"Much obliged," Wolfe replied. He watched the two men as they prepared the boat, checking the nets and fishing setups.

Rusty pointed at a bench on the rear deck. "Soon as we get out of the harbor, you will need to cut bait. We got some leftovers from yesterday. Slice and dice, and we'll load up the hooks. Sometimes we will hit schools that act like they never ate before. Other times, you have to bribe them to take the food. In the end, we always win because the captain is the best fisherman in the bay."

"I did not pay him to say that," the captain replied proudly. Wolfe started helping with Rusty's tasks, the ones that looked to be the most menial. Hard work never hurt anyone, least of all Jim Wolfe. He scrubbed the deck between jobs. Rusty went below into the small cabin. He fired up the stove and made coffee.

"Real coffee?" Wolfe asked, leaning through the open hatch.

"Best in the fleet," Rusty replied.

"Is everything on this boat the best in the fleet?"

"Pretty much." Rusty laughed. He put out the fire and headed topside when the captain yelled to cast off. Between the two deckhands, they pushed away from the pier. The captain engaged the propeller and guided the boat toward the deeper harbor. The captain looped the vessel around and back toward the shore where a boat was moored. Hands were working the deck, getting it ready to go to sea.

"Ahoy!" the captain called.

"Ahoy! Is that you, Ahab? Worst ship in the fleet," someone shouted back.

"Your mother was pelican bait!" the captain barked but slowed his boat to come alongside.

"Damn. I was right. Ahab and the *White Whale*. Need some fishing tips?" the captain of the bigger boat joked.

"Got a new deckhand from Florida. He wants to know what you have seen down that way. Wolfe?"

Jim leaned over the rail. "I just want to know."

"Sorry to disappoint you, mister, but that whole area is a waste. The whole bay glows and is still polluting the ocean. We have gone close enough to see there is nothing left for twenty miles in any direction. The big bridge over the bay? That is gone. Everything is rubble and dust."

Wolfe had heard that before, but *Sallie Mae's* captain was not flapping his gums just to hear himself speak. He had turned serious when talking about Tampa Bay.

"I understand," Wolfe said, his jaw muscles tightening

with the tension of the realization. Was this the closure he sought?

No. He still had to go. Enough had survived to tell the story, and they had gone somewhere. On the other hand, if the destruction was as complete as the captain described, maybe they hadn't suffered.

"Will you be going that way anytime soon?" Wolfe asked.

"No reason to. The ocean is spoiled. It's destroyed, land and sea. Let it go, mister, or you'll twist yourself into knots. We've all lost people. It's time to move on."

"Thank you for your time and information," Wolfe replied, looking away quickly and getting back to work fussing with the fishing rigs.

The two captains let the silence linger for too long before wishing each other well. His captain steered the ship toward the middle of the bay.

"Taking a short one today," he shouted to his crew. "Let's get some fish and then call it an early day. Tomorrow, we'll go after bigger prey."

Wolfe kept his head bowed as he tried to work through what he was thinking. When it turned light and they sent the nets into the water, he was all business.

CHAPTER NINE

"I ain't never seen no man pull a net like that," Rusty said, awe in his voice as he and the captain watched Wolfe manhandle the net back into the boat. Rusty had been in the way, and Wolfe asked him to step aside as he used the whole deck to pull and stack.

Their steam winch had failed, and the net was full of the day's catch. They would not cut the net free, and leaving the catch behind was at the bottom of the list. That left pulling it in by hand.

Wolfe showed them it was nothing but a normal hard day's work. Hand over hand, he pulled, dragging the net and fish into the boat.

"I think he does a better job than the winch," the captain pondered.

They stayed out of the way until the bulk of the fish were in the boat before jumping in to help move the catch into the cooler compartment below. When it was done and the net rolled tightly, the captain looked at the sun.

"Can you do that one more time?" he asked.

Wolfe shrugged. "Sure. If there is work to do, let us do it."

The captain raced to the wheel and spun it around. "Roll out the boom and send it out."

Rusty unpinned the boom and angled it over the side. He prepared to let the spool run free to deploy the net. When the captain nodded, Rusty released the lock, and the net unrolled into the ocean. The captain made a slow turn, and when the last of the net dropped off the spool, Rusty made sure it was secure.

With both ends of the line in the boat, all they had to do was watch Jim Wolfe pull it in.

Wolf finished eating a sandwich made of fried fish, lettuce, and thin slices of bread, spread with a generous layer of tartar sauce. It almost tasted like the old days, but the bread was off. Their problem with grains would continue for a while—years probably before they figured out something that worked. Wolfe was okay with it. The meals he and Jennifer were getting were good. All he had to do was pay a few scrip for them.

That meant working, and he had no problem with a hard day's work.

But it did not get him any closer to Bradenton. He put his back to the sun and looked east. Over there. That was where he needed to go.

"Let us see what you got, Jim! Bring it in, and maybe today will be our best day ever."

Wolfe did not bother acknowledging the captain. He simply took the ends of the net and started pulling them in. He moved closer to the stern to brace one leg while he pulled to keep himself from being yanked overboard. After five minutes, he was sweating like an overworked mule. Rusty used the hand crank to roll the net back onto the spool once it was in the boat. That kept the deck mostly clear.

"Drink!" he shouted over his shoulder. Rusty appeared with a jug to pour water into Wolfe's mouth. "Much obliged."

When the net rose to the surface, thrashing and splashing signaled a problem. Wolfe did not know what it was, but the captain knew. He moved to the deck and put his hand on Wolfe's shoulder.

"It looks like it is not meant to be. Let it go and dump the net," the captain ordered.

"Why? It is almost in. Just a little bit more."

"That there is a tiger shark. A maneater. You keep hauling, and he'll destroy my net, and the fish will escape all the same. No way we can drag him in the boat. Someone is likely to get hurt, and then we will lose the fish."

"I think there is another way," Wolfe said. He turned to Rusty. "Tighten it up and lock the winch."

Rusty did as he was told. The captain shook his head. "Let it go."

Wolfe pulled his shirt off and threw it aside. He took the all-purpose knife from the slot next to the fishing rigs and ran toward the stern.

"No!" the captain called, but it was too late.

Wolfe dove over the back and into the frenzy that was a twelve-foot tiger shark flailing within a too-weak fishing net.

With a smooth entry, staying close to the surface, Wolfe kept his eyes on the beast. It thrashed wildly, not noticing that it was the target of a new predator. Fish darted and bounced off while he closed with the shark.

Without the leverage of something solid under his feet, Wolfe was at a disadvantage. He counted on his arm strength. With unerring precision, he thrust the knife into the shark's head. It jammed against the bone and became lodged. The shark went wild. Wolfe tried to grab its snout and lower jaw to keep the jagged teeth away from his fragile skin, but he slipped and could not get a grip.

The first slash across his chest twisted him and almost threw a leg into the creature's mouth. Blood poured out and saltwater poured in, burning like molten metal. The two came out of the water. Wolfe raised his fist and hammered down harder than any human had ever driven a fist before. Stunned, the shark stopped its wild gyrations.

Wolfe kicked hard to get past the mouth. He dug one hand into the gills and tossed a leg across the broad back, then pulled his knife free while straddling the beast. He rose up and drove downward. Three times he jammed the knife into the dark gray head, and the last snapped the blade. The shark deflated as its life ended. Wolfe tossed the handle over his shoulder.

Wolfe continued to straddle the creature, buoyed by the crush of fish beneath. In the boat, the captain and Rusty waved at Wolfe to come aboard. Finally, Wolfe pushed off and swam ahead. Two eager hands reached down to grab him and pull him in.

Wolfe grimaced from the pain across his chest. "If you do not mind a little pain, I have something that will close that up for you." The captain disappeared into the cabin, returning shortly with a staple gun. Wolfe looked at it without changing his expression.

"Go ahead, Ahab. We have fish to bring aboard." Wolfe clenched his teeth in anticipation of the staples snapping through his skin to close the wound.

CHAPTER TEN

Jim leaned back while the captain poured his precious moonshine across the wound. Rusty was cleaning up the deck. The small fishing trawler lumbered through the water, full to the gills. The tiger shark hung from the boom, its tail flopping across the deck at the crest of each wave.

"That was the craziest thing I ever seen."

Wolfe did not reply. The pain faded with time. Only the first twenty minutes had been excruciating. After the first few applications of moonshine, the pain dulled.

"There," the captain declared. He threw back the last mouthful, wincing before he swallowed. "The good stuff."

Wolfe nodded. He had not been much for drinking, but events suggested today was a good day for a stiff one.

"And Jim, do not do that again. If you got caught in the net and dragged under, even your strength could not save you." The captain looked out the window at the sun above the horizon. "Thirty minutes of sunlight left. We should be in the harbor by then. I tell you what. Take tomorrow off and then come the next day. Let us take a trip along the coast to the east, see where that takes us."

Wolfe contemplated the offer before nodding. "Sounds good. I thank you."

"No. I am thanking you. The biggest haul ever for the *White Whale*, and we are bringing a tiger shark home, too."

"Can you eat that?"

"Nah, but it will make decent chum."

"So you can catch more sharks?"

"Now you understand!" The captain clapped Wolfe on the back.

Wolfe did not understand at all, but they did not call the captain Ahab for no reason.

Jennifer and Buddy were waiting on the shore as the *White Whale* cruised toward the dock. Wolfe waved. The highlight of his day was coming home. He wondered if the young girl had selected a place to eat. He could use something hot that stuck to his ribs.

She waved back and Buddy barked, wagging his big hairy tail. He panted heavily. That was a constant the whole time they traveled through the Deep South in the summer. Even in the early evening, it was warm. The bugs were out, but a light breeze kept the worst of the insects at bay.

Once docked, a crew from the processing plant rolled their carts down to the shore.

"Gonna need more than that!" the captain yelled cheerfully. The man in front waved him away as if he always claimed a huge catch.

Five minutes later, he agreed. "Looks like a three-trip night. We are going to be buried until morning." It did not sound like a complaint. Too much work was a good problem to have. It was all paid time. The foreman from the shop watched the carts trundle back and forth.

"Sixteen full carts. What about the shark?"

"Are you buying?"

"I fancy myself a taxidermist. I think I could stuff that and hang it out front. We will have the best front display out of everyone. Will you take five scrip for it?"

"Deal!" the captain declared, offering his hand to seal the arrangement.

"Three times sixteen plus five equals fifty-three scrip. Damn! I only brought fifty."

The captain waited. The agreement was for fifty-three. The foreman was trying to get the captain to concede the three. He had no intention of doing that. Those belonged to Jim Wolfe, without whom there would be no shark or record haul.

"Fine." The foreman smiled. "I had to try." He pulled a small notebook out of his pocket and wrote an IOU for the extra three. "I will be able to pay that tomorrow if you stop by."

"Consider it done. We are taking tomorrow off and then making a bit of a long haul. Might be gone a week. See if we can bring in some tuna or better cuts. The good people of Mobile deserve a treat."

The two shook hands once again. The captain left the shark to the foreman, who could figure out how to get it to the warehouse.

"Jim!" the captain called, waving at Rusty to join them on the shore. Wolfe stood with Miss Jennifer by his side and Buddy leaning against her. "Good job today." He handed over twenty-five scrip—a week's worth of wages for a single day's work.

He gave Rusty his five scrip and kept the last twenty to keep the boat running. He planned to split the last three evenly whenever he collected them.

"Thanks, Ahab," Wolfe replied.

"That is not my real name," the captain countered.

"You never told me your real name. Ahab not good enough?"

The captain chuckled and nodded. He pointed at Wolfe and walked away with Rusty in tow. The crew from the warehouse returned with three carts to wrestle the shark off the boat. Jennifer watched Wolfe to see if he would offer to help. He did not. He was done working. His chest ached and it was leaking, leaving a bloody stain on his shirt.

"Are you okay?" Jennifer asked.

"I will be fine, Miss Jennifer. Did you find a place for us to eat?"

"I have, and I hope you like it." She smiled broadly. Wolfe frowned. He knew what was coming. "We're going to Carlisle's home to meet his family."

Yep. That was it.

CHAPTER ELEVEN

Wolfe steeled his nerve during the short walk to Jennifer's boyfriend's house. He had changed his shirt, but when Jennifer saw the staples, she had insisted on a proper stitching. With two pliers and Mister Keaton's help, they removed them one by one while stitching up the wound behind them. Jennifer's steady hand kept the stitches tight, while Keaton kept taking drinks of a bottle that smelled suspiciously of cheap whiskey.

"Talk of that shark is already running up and down the bay. You jumped into the net to kill a twelve-foot tiger with a filleting knife? You are a legend, Mister Wolfe."

Jennifer cocked one eyebrow at him, not amused by the risk he had taken. "Uh-huh," she muttered.

"We needed the fish," Wolfe found himself explaining before shrugging it off. Three more staples removed and a little more suturing, and the deed was done. The jagged eight-inch slice was closed.

"I am certain I would not let someone staple my chest," Keaton remarked, making a sour face as he looked at the pile of bloody staples. He turned to Jennifer. "But you do good work. We need more of that around here."

"There are that many people as brave and stupid as Mister Wolfe?" Jennifer asked evenly.

Keaton started to laugh. Behind his welding goggles, Wolfe hid his expression. He did not want to share how much Miss Jennifer had sounded like Lurleen at that moment, as if the young girl had been raised by his wife. The foreman continued to laugh as Jennifer tied off the last knot, giving an extra tug to reinforce her statement. Wolfe winced.

"That is my daughter," Wolfe said proudly. "Let me get cleaned up. I guess I have a boy to meet."

Jennifer's expression lightened. She and Keaton left the bathroom to Wolfe, who never tired of a shower. It was one of the things he had missed the most in the new world.

When he finished, he found Jennifer waiting. She had laid out his jeans, which had been cleaned and a new shirt. He gave her all his scrip each day. She managed the money side of it and did not take that lightly. It helped her pay attention to her math classes. She had even written a budget to help her manage their daily costs and save for a rainy day.

Meeting her boyfriend must have qualified for spending from their savings. Wolfe slowly shook his head as he dressed. An old but clean button-down shirt. He wondered if she had borrowed it or bought it second-hand.

Wolfe hefted his pack onto his shoulder, the rifle broken down within and the bow tied to the side.

"We are not bringing that."

Wolfe started to argue, but decided discretion was the better part of valor. He pushed the pack under his bed. There were no problems with theft. The people had come to an understanding with each other, trust that made scrip hold its value and kept homes safe.

Buddy did not like the short delay in leaving. He was

ready to go out after having been cooped up in the room. Jennifer took him to school with her, but after they returned to their quarters, they did not go out.

The big dog preferred life on the road, where he could wander and hunt on his own. He also had not gotten used to a diet that consisted mostly of fish.

As they walked, Wolfe told Jennifer what was up. "Tomorrow I am off, but the day after, we are taking the *White Whale* and heading to Florida. I will ask Mister Keaton to check in on you."

Jennifer was instantly angry. "Buddy and I are going with you!" she declared, stamping a small foot wearing a new shoe. Wolfe had not noticed that she was wearing a dress with patent leather shoes. They were not new, either. He expected she bought them at the same place she'd found his shirt.

"There is no room onboard for more than the captain, Rusty, and me. We will go take a look and then come back. I will come back to you."

"Fine."

Wolfe knew that word never meant "fine." He had been there the whole time his daughter was becoming an adult, and he had missed it. He needed to improve his parenting so he could cope.

"I will stay with Carlisle and his parents. They will have me."

Wolfe stopped and stood, mouth agape. "N-no!" he stammered.

"Then Carlisle will come stay with me. There really are only two choices," she explained and started walking again.

"No," Wolfe repeated. His mind raced, looking for a different answer. "You stay in the apartment with Buddy and no one else. You'll see Carlisle at school." Wolfe was back to not liking the boyfriend.

"Okay," she said too easily. "You'll be gone, so I will have to make the best decisions for me."

"No," Wolfe said weakly. "I will talk to the captain and see how we can bring you two on board. You do not take up much space, but Buddy is going to be in the way."

"We are not leaving him!"

Wolfe tried to calm her. "I did not say we were leaving him. It is going to be a rough trip, and we all could suffer if we are not prepared."

He did not want her to go because of the radiation and the trials of being on the ocean for days, but what he feared most was what they would find. Would it be better for Wolfe to have Jennifer with him when he learned the truth, no matter what that was? The trials of his life were coming to a peak. His heart beat faster just thinking about it. Showing weakness in front of his daughter was not something he wanted to do, even though he was impressed by her sewing skills, stitching up his shark bite.

She was growing up too fast.

They had not walked far, most of it in silence. Wolfe's mind was busy with the events of the day and the way forward. The one thing the last four years taught him was to take his time and think things through. He thought he had the patience of a nomad but found that was not true. He had patience when it was just him and things were going his way.

Jennifer stopped and pointed at a nondescript wooden home that looked like most of its neighbors. He did not know what he had expected. For Jim Wolfe, things were moving too fast. He did not have enough time to think about anything. Jennifer left him standing there while she and Buddy headed for the door.

Wolfe sighed heavily and started walking, his feet suddenly weighing more than they should have, his legs responding sluggishly. He forced himself to walk upright and maintain a steady stride. His head started to swim.

Before Jennifer reached the door, it opened, and a woman Wolfe's age stepped out. With dark hair and dark eyes beneath long lashes, she smiled radiantly. A man, younger and taller, with broad shoulders, joined her on the stoop. He wrapped an arm around her waist and waved. Jennifer greeted them both.

Normal people. Wolfe looked at himself, with the welding goggles and his hair returning to its post-war white color. He touched the goggles, which added to his odd appearance.

"I think I should go," he whispered to Jennifer. She reached out like a rattlesnake and took him by the hand, almost dragging him to the front door.

"Mister and Mrs. Stanton, this is my father, Mister Jim Wolfe." She curtsied.

Wolfe tipped his chin. "Pleased to make your acquaintance. I will not be able to stay, but I am happy to have met you. You look like decent folk."

"You're staying," Jennifer said a little too loudly before looking at the ground. "Please."

A young man appeared. He looked like his pa. He was tall already, taller than Wolfe, but the young face gave away his age. The young man would grow into his shoulders, but presently, he was a bit trim. Probably needed more than fish if he wanted to bulk up.

"You must be Carlisle," Wolfe said, offering his hand.

"Yes, sir," he said, taking Wolfe's hand and giving it his strongest shake. He had a ways to go. Wolfe let him know in a subtle way that he wasn't there yet. It was also a mild warning that Jennifer's dad was not up for games.

It ended quickly, and Wolfe smiled.

Jennifer tapped him on the arm. "Please?"

"You two go inside. We will be along shortly," Wolfe told

her. Jennifer and Carlisle held hands as they hurried inside. Buddy ran after them. Wolfe turned to the Stantons. "We were stuck out west for a long spell before being able to travel this way. My wife and son were in Bradenton, and I have to see for myself. We leave day after tomorrow, and I have a favor to ask. Will you look after my daughter and her dog for the short time I will be gone? She has grown so fast, and I am not very good at parenting."

"Call me Renata, and this is Carl," she drawled. "Do not beat yourself up over nothing. You have done a marvelous job. We have never met a finer young lady. You lived in the wastelands?"

"The red zone where the wilders live. We had to fight our way through them, but it is much nicer here. I appreciate every day where someone is not trying to kill me."

Renata's eyes shot wide and her hand flew to her chest. "My stars!"

Her husband laughed. "Me, too, but there is a lot less of that here. Come on in. We picked up some fresh stuff right out of the greenhouse. I expect you do not have to go, do you?" He tipped his head back enough to look at Wolfe with a critical eye. "I cannot imagine how hard it is to be a man with a teenage daughter." He pointed to his eyes and then pointed to Wolfe's goggles. "I get you."

Renata playfully pushed her husband. "Of course, we will be more than happy to have Jennifer stay here while you are gone. Come on now. I'm sure dinner is either on fire or getting cold."

Carl hurried ahead to hold the door for his wife and their guest.

Wolfe felt the strain lift from his shoulders. He realized that he was at his limit on things to worry about. Leaving Jennifer in good hands freed him to focus on the broken world before him.

CHAPTER TWELVE

Carlisle had arrived at the warehouse before dawn to help Jennifer move her things to his house. They joined Wolfe at the dock to wave goodbye. She did not need any help with her things since she had been carrying them for a thousand miles. Wolfe did not have much to say about it other than to see her make her own way.

Wolfe had his pack and all his possessions with him. The warehouse apartment was empty, and they had left it spotless. Keaton said they were welcome back anytime. Best tenants he had ever had.

The boat slipped smoothly through the calm early-morning Gulf waters. The steam engine made enough noise to disrupt the serenity of the dawn, but it was a necessary sound. It made travel possible. The captain had loaded up firewood the day prior, ensuring the boat was ready for a long journey. He also had a two-man saw, two axes, and a maul. They would have to stop somewhere along the way to acquire water and more fuel.

The captain said they would be within sight of the coastline nearly the whole way.

Wolfe waved at his daughter and her companions. He was sure of one thing—he needed to do this alone. For everything else, he would have to count on others. Mobile was a safe place, a place to raise a family. Maybe if he found Lurleen and JoJo, he would bring them back.

If only.

The crew of the *White Whale* took the opportunity to troll, using short poles with heavy line. They had stocked some food but expected to catch fish as they went. The *Whale* was a fishing boat, after all.

Wolfe handed his pole to Rusty and joined the captain at the wheel. "If we go ashore along the way, I can hunt for us, maybe get some red meat."

"Gators down here, Jim. You would have to go inland a ways."

"Gator is not bad eating."

The captain looked Wolfe up and down. "You are a country boy at heart, Jim Wolfe, willing to eat a little bit of everything but not a lot of one thing." The captain steered into a wave and held his heading to keep from getting buffeted by the swells. "I miss biscuits and gravy."

"And grits," Wolfe added.

"Fish on!" Rusty shouted. Wolfe jumped into action to relieve Rusty of the second pole, reeling in the line so it would not tangle the first. This was survival fishing. One never wanted to risk losing a fish once hooked.

Rusty cheered and yelled into the ship's wake. He stood with his legs braced and fought the fisherman's fight from time immemorial, giving up line when needed and reeling in a frenzy when the fish darted toward the boat. The massive treble hook held, and the fight continued.

Wolfe put his rig inside the boat and snatched the dip net, keeping it low so the fish could not see it. Holding the rod high, he let it absorb much of the back and forth during the fight. The pole bent in half before straightening and bouncing. He reeled each time it came up, letting the line peel off with the drag. He dialed it back a little at a time, making it harder and harder for the fish to run.

Rusty used his core muscles to lift, reel, and coax the fish closer to the boat, but the man was tiring. His arms shook as he tried to reel.

A fin broke the surface, and then a tail splashed hard as it fought. The captain started shouting and cheering. "Get him, Rusty!"

"What is it?" Wolfe asked. He set the net down and held onto Rusty, one hand on the pole to keep it from slipping away.

"A bluefin tuna, and it is a monster!" the captain yelled over his shoulder. He slowed the boat until it was barely moving.

"Take it," Rusty gasped. The fish tried to drag the rig overboard during the handover. If it had not been for Wolfe's magnificent strength, he would have lost the pole and the fish. He held the monster with one hand before setting himself in place. The burst of energy quickly faded, and Wolfe reeled him in, one smooth crank after another.

Rusty panted like a dog, rubbing at his stiff arms. "Take the wheel," the captain said.

The two changed places.

"Only you can pull that thing into the boat," the captain said. "You grab the gaff, and I will take the pole. Careful now."

They took their time shifting the rod. When the captain had it firmly in his grip, he started cranking. The fish made a dash toward the boat.

"Starboard!" the captain called to Rusty. Instead of letting the fish get ahead of the boat, they kept the stern toward it. The fin broke the surface as it passed.

Like a bolt of lightning, Wolfe slashed the gaff into the creature's head, twisted the point home, and pulled back. The fish came up and out of the water. When it landed inside the boat, it was already dead from being gaffed through its brain.

"Not the usual way, but the fish is in the boat. What do you think, Rusty? Five hundred pounds?"

"Easy!" Rusty kicked the boat to a fast idle and joined the others on the deck. "That is some good eating right there."

Wolfe did not see anything special besides how big the fish was. The captain immediately cut into it and fileted a small part. He looked at the pinkish-red meat with slight white marbling before putting it into his mouth.

"That is good," he said. "Well done, Rusty!"

The captain handed a piece to the deckhand, who ate it without hesitation.

"Butcher this thing and put the meat on ice. We are going to eat like kings and then some on this trip. I will kick her into high gear since we do not need to fish anymore."

The captain offered Wolfe a piece of the tuna.

"Go on and eat it. Back in the old days, this would have been a-few-hundred-dollars-a-pound sashimi. I fished in the before time and never saw anything like this. It would have made my whole year."

Wolfe sampled the piece. It was okay, better than any of the fish he had had back in town, but not as good as a steak. He clapped the captain on the back. "Since there is nothing else, this will have to do."

The captain smiled and visited the boiler to stoke the fire, check the water, and return to the wheel. He adjusted the steam to drive the propeller to higher RPMs. The boat turned due east, starting to bounce as it powered through the chop on its way to Tampa Bay.

The *White Whale* sailed fast the rest of that day before Wolfe's fingertips started to tingle. He held his hand toward the shore.

"It is a red zone over there. You might want to go farther out to sea."

The captain spun the wheel and headed for the open ocean.

"That there is Pensacola, and up ahead is Fort Walton Beach. Over the horizon is Panama City. They all got hit hard."

The Navy, Air Force, and Army all had bases in that stretch. It would have been a prime target.

"I am taking us a little past Panama City. I hope that area is clear, and since you can feel the radiation, we will know for sure. We will need to restock our firewood and load up with fresh water. This old steam engine will work until the cows come home, but even at the top end, we only get ten knots, and usually it is more like eight." The captain began a string of creative curses harsh enough to peel paint while simultaneously caressing her wood, begging for a little more speed.

The captain talked to the ship like she was an ex-wife but treated her like a new lover.

"How far is Bradenton?" Wolfe asked.

"Three hundred miles, maybe three-fifty from Mobile. This old tub is good, but I do not want to get caught in the middle of the Gulf in case weather comes up or worse, we run out of firewood. If we stock up well when we stop, we might be able to shoot straight down there. If we get a red sky at night, that is."

"Is that real?"

"One hundred percent." The captain winked and turned his attention back to the gauges that told him how the steam engine was operating. It was a simple system, but complex if

one wanted to get the most from it without blowing themselves up.

CHAPTER THIRTEEN

"Keep a good lookout!" the captain yelled as if Rusty did not know why he crouched over the bow looking through the water in front of the boat. "Saint Vincent Island. Once past this, we'll be in protected waters. Up ahead is East Bay. On the eastern side of that used to be a hundred docks where folks had their boats. All depends what happened to them, but we might find a spot. Lots of trees in those yards. And then up around the bend, there are a few streams we may be able to tap into for fresh water."

Wolfe watched for movement, looking for signs that humanity had returned to the area. Or game. Despite the captain's claims about the value of the tuna, Wolfe longed for red meat. He held his hand outside the cabin to check for residual radiation. He could not sense any, and that was a good sign. Wisps of hot areas had come with the wind over the past forty miles. Wolfe was glad to be past it.

Florida had been on the front lines of an intercontinental war. The scars would run deep for decades, if not longer.

They passed under a bay bridge that was still intact. "That is a good sign," the captain declared, but he craned his neck to see the structure before running the *White Whale* beneath its tallest span.

Inside the bay, the residential area with the docks was heavily overgrown. Over half the docks remained in place, with too many dead ships still attached.

"There's one," Rusty said, hatcheting an arm in the direction before pointing to shallows and guiding the boat in. He was ready when the boat bumped the dock. He jumped from the deck and landed solidly on the wood of the dock, breaking it and disappearing into the water below. Wolfe jumped forward and leaned over, grabbing a piling to stop the *White Whale*'s forward momentum. He looked at the breakthrough. Rusty was already up with a hand on the next board.

"That sucked," the deckhand sputtered before pulling himself out of the water and onto the dock. He bent down to look at the remaining wood. "Well, I'll be. Those were the only two bad boards on this thing." He carefully stepped from one to the next until he reached the shore. Then he backtracked to help Wolfe tie off the boat.

Wolfe entered the cabin and rummaged through his backpack until he had the parts of his trusty AR-15. He put them together and slapped the magazine into place. He pulled the charging handle back and let it go, watching it send a 5.56mm round into the chamber, then slung it over his shoulder and headed on deck.

"You had that thing, and we fought to gaff the tuna?" the captain exclaimed.

"There was no fight to gaff the tuna." Wolfe locked eyes with the captain and added, "Ammunition is scarce."

"Knowing you have a rifle changes how we can bring big fish into the boat. For example, a shark that's trying to shred the net. Next time, Jim, just shoot it."

Wolfe chuckled. "Next time, I will."

He stepped onto the dock on his way ashore while the captain yelled at Rusty to break out the tools to cut firewood.

Once into the overgrown brush, Wolfe unslung his rifle and carried it with two hands. The wild was reclaiming the land without any sign of humanity. Wolfe hoped a wild boar or deer would make its presence known.

He passed a collapsed house and made it to a road that was not completely overgrown. If he turned right, it would take him back to the coast. If he turned left, it would take him away from the small community. He turned left and started to run along the road, covering a short distance quickly before he found an outlet that led away from the houses. Soon, the brush was too heavy to run through.

Wolfe forced his way ahead, eyes on the muddy ground, looking for animal tracks. There were indications of plenty of birds and small game, but nothing bigger. He continued for a mile and then a second before he ran out of road. That was when the terrain became too difficult to keep going. He turned around to head back and spotted a movement out of the corner of his eye.

He froze, turning his head at a glacially slow speed to not spook whatever he had seen. He waited and watched.

Another movement. In the trees above. Not a bird. Wolfe relaxed when he saw it was a monkey. "Did you escape from a zoo? Good for you, my friend. Enjoy the freedom. You deserve it." Wolfe slung his rifle. Without a single sign of bigger game, he resigned himself to eating three-hundred-dollar-a-pound bluefin tuna. He laughed at that, thinking about what he had eaten for the first two years after the bombs fell. Protein bars. And what he had eaten in the red zones afterward, which was anything to keep him alive.

It was not such a great sacrifice after all, Wolfe decided. He retraced his steps, stopping when he reached the neighborhood. If no one had gone through the area, maybe something remained if the people never returned once they'd evacuated.

He kicked in the door of the first house. A quick stroll through showed him that whoever had lived there had left in a hurry. A desk had its drawers open. A charging cable for a computer remained on top, but the notebook was gone. Important papers and equipment filled other drawers. In the kitchen, the cupboards were mostly full. The stock of canned goods made his mouth water. Wolfe looked for a bag, finding a stash of plastic grocery bags stuffed into another grocery bag. He smiled. It was what Lurleen used to do.

He filled as many bags as he could before checking out the remainder of the home. It was a family's house. Pictures of better days hung on the walls. In the master bedroom, he found that the owner was a bigger man than Wolfe, much bigger. The teenaged son was more his size. Wolfe traded jeans for a pair that had been neatly folded in a drawer for the past four years. He decided to take a second pair and a few of the boy's shirts.

Socks were nirvana, and in a closet by the front door, he found a pair of combat boots with soles intact, unlike his, which he had repaired more than once. He put on a pair of musty but clean socks and then pulled on the new boots.

When he was changed out, he picked up the bags and headed back to the boat. The sound of sawing led him in the direction of his shipmates. He found them using the two-man saw to make quick work of old deadfall. Wolfe could not be sure that it had not been someone's driftwood yard display. They did not need it, not anymore.

Wolfe put the canned goods on a heavily rusted metal picnic table. He took one can out and showed it to the captain.

"Baked beans. I can get behind those!" He laughed at his own joke before getting back to cutting the wood. Wolfe picked up the axe and started splitting the larger pieces. With single strokes, he finished the task quickly. He took the axe to more deadfall, and soon they had a respectable pile of wood to burn.

"There are monkeys in the woods out there." Wolfe pointed before he picked up the bags.

"Monkeys? They better not get on my boat." The captain wiped the sweat from his brow and hurriedly gathered an armload of wood. Rusty followed suit, and the three men walked quickly to the bay side of the houses. Wolfe stopped abruptly and dropped his bags. He held up his hand for the others to stop, but they didn't see until they ran into him.

Wolfe pulled his rifle from his shoulder and took careful aim. He fired, and the crocodile that had crawled ashore and was waiting between them and the dock flopped twice and laid still. Wolfe took three steps closer and fired again.

Just to be sure. He held the rifle in his hands as he carefully scanned the water, looking for a ripple or a bump that should not have been there.

"You mean I went into water that has crocs?" Rusty said, fear tingeing his voice.

"Get that firewood aboard. I will watch," Wolfe told them.

The captain shrugged. "Good shooting."

They continued down the dock to where the *White Whale* waited. It took only a couple of seconds to determine that the creatures had not made it aboard.

"I heard from folks who plied the Caribbean that monkeys will mess your boat up bad," the captain said. "One of us needs to stay aboard to make sure they don't get out here, and to keep watch to make sure we do not get any more gators."

"I will do it. I need to clean that beast. Ever had croc tail?"

"Good eating," Rusty confirmed. The captain nodded.

"Between that and the bluefin, it is like I have died and

gone to heaven. Are you going to cook it, too? We will cut some extra wood for a fire. Chop, chop, Rusty! We got work to do."

"What about fresh water?" Wolfe asked.

"We will have to head up an inlet or two to find a fast-running stream. We passed five of them on the west side of the bay. I'm not worried. Then we'll put the hose into it and man the pumps. If it is a slow mover, it will be polluted with salt water. We will find something with a good current, hopefully before we ground the boat."

Wolfe nodded. He dumped the groceries into the boat and returned to the gator. He dragged it to the back porch of the once-fine home. There was a fire pit, filled with weeds but surrounded by brick. He tore out the weeds and kicked away the debris. He pulled his combat knife and got to work on the gator, butchering it to get the most meat from it. When he was done, he hauled the carcass back to the water and tossed it in as a warning to other gators in the area.

Or it could draw gators. If you saw one, there were more, just like cockroaches. He kept his eyes open. When he got back to the pit, Rusty was there with an armload of wood. He dumped it to the side. "You ever kill a croc with your bare hands?"

"Gator, yes. Croc, no." Wolfe replied.

"Of course you have." Rusty looked impressed. "I am not worried as long as you are with us. You must have had a rough time in the waste of whatever is left of America."

Wolfe did not answer. He focused on starting the fire and getting it going, along with finding what he would need to cook the croc. He glanced over his shoulder. A large house sat behind him. It looked untouched, like the other home he had been in. Wolfe looked at his new clothes and boots. "I will be right back. Watch out for monkeys and crocs and anything else that would steal our dinner. I need to find a pan. Or a spit."

He pushed the French doors open. They were stiff from being swollen by the humidity, but they were not locked. He strolled through the house, which was stifling from the trapped humidity. The floor was soft in spots where the wood was starting to rot. In the kitchen, he found everything he needed, including a set of three high-end Japanese kitchen knives. He helped himself to those to replace the one he had broken off in the shark's head.

"I will call when dinner is ready," Wolfe told him. Rusty grumbled a little before walking away to join the captain in restocking the wood for the boat's boiler.

After the fire had flared and settled into a smoother burn, Wolfe put the tail on a metal rack above the heat. He watched it cook, wondering how close he was to Lurleen and JoJo. Could he run there quicker than the boat could sail? It nagged at him and made the cooking and firewood cutting slow to an agonizing pace.

It was time for Wolfe to be home.

CHAPTER FOURTEEN

Across the bay, the second river they tried flowed quickly enough to keep the water fresh. They powered into the outlet and hung a hose over the side. Wolfe manually spun the pump so quickly that it started to heat up. The captain chased Wolfe off the job, letting Rusty do it so he would not burn out the equipment. It only took a half-hour, after which Rusty was soaked with sweat. Wolfe scowled at the bay and the morning sun. It was hard to tell whether the sky was red through his welding goggles.

The captain kept glancing at it but did not seem concerned. He slowed the RPMs and let the current push him backward. Rusty shouted directions from the aft deck while Wolfe put the pump and hose away. On command, the captain spun the wheel to turn the boat toward the Gulf. He increased the steam to maximum, grinning as the *White Whale* responded with a surge through the protected waters. She ran quickly under the bridge, across an inlet, and into the open waters.

They headed southeast. Wolfe watched the land receding behind them. There was no land in sight to either side.

"Less than two hundred miles on a straight shot. We should reach Tampa first thing in the morning as long as we hold this heading."

Wolfe started to breathe faster. Tomorrow. He had been traveling a long time to get to this point. He could not believe it, but would there be a resolution? He clenched his jaw and watched the water ahead.

The whitecaps seemed to come out of nowhere, buffeting the fishing boat, tossing it like a cork in a whirlpool. The captain turned the boat due east and headed for what he thought was the nearest land.

"Man the bilge!" he shouted over the rising roar of the angry ocean. Wolfe put his back into it, turning the crank and pumping the errant sea overboard, but for every turn, more seemed to enter the boat. He braced himself and redoubled his efforts, focusing on nothing but turning the crank to keep the boat from foundering. Rusty dodged back and forth, following the captain's orders while Ahab fought with keeping the boiler stocked and the boat on a straight line.

Waves crashed over the rails, threatening to throw the hands overboard. The captain shut the door on the small pilot's cabin of the fishing boat, locking Wolfe and Rusty outside. They knew he had no choice.

Like a machine, Wolfe powered the bilge pump, refusing to slow down despite the violent attack on the *White Whale.* Then the rain started and the skies darkened. The darkness was shattered by the lightning, explosions that made Wolfe wince and see stars. He continued to turn the crank, ducking his head out of the deluge.

Rusty lashed himself to the ladder leading to the open top

over the pilot's cabin. He screamed in terror. Wolfe had to hang on to the rail with one hand and crouch to keep from being swept overboard while continuing to fight.

The captain opened the door and yelled, "Wolfe, I need you! Rusty, take the bilge pump."

Rusty unlashed himself but held onto the rope, and when he reached Wolfe, he tied himself down. He started cranking as quickly as he could, but it was a pale shadow of what Wolfe had been doing.

Inside with the captain, he found the man blinking and squinting through the front window. "Cannot see a damn thing. Can you?"

Wolfe looked ahead. In between lightning bolts, he removed his goggles quickly to see the way ahead. Towering waves occupied the space between sea and sky. "It is not good," Wolfe replied.

"You drive. Compass says east. Hold that course!" Before Wolfe could answer, the captain had slipped out the door to join Rusty at the bilge pump.

Wolfe had been paying attention, but he had not practiced driving the boat, which also meant controlling the boiler and the steam. No time like the present. Wolfe looked at it, trying to remember why the captain had made the adjustments he did and when. He touched nothing while fighting to turn the boat straight into the incoming waves to keep them from capsizing. The propeller screamed when it came out of the water as the *Whale* crested the peak before racing into the trough beyond. Wolfe pulled his goggles away for half a second at a time, knowing that if lightning caught him unprotected, he'd be blinded, maybe permanently.

He fought the wheel and the waves ahead, snatching glimpses through one squinted eye. The ocean had become an unforgiving bronco doing its best to buck the fishermen from its back before trampling them into the ground.

The captain returned, checked the steam, made a minor adjustment, and rushed back out. Wolfe did not even have time to ask him any questions. The two men fought the bilge for another spell before Rusty came inside.

"Captain says you need to spot us. We are about dead."

"There is enough lightning. You can see what you need. I will take care of the pump, and you two keep us heading toward shore. I am not a good swimmer!"

Despite the threat to their lives, Rusty laughed. "We will do our best, Jim," he promised, crossing himself for added emphasis.

Wolfe took his spot at the pump and started cranking. The water volume increased as if Wolfe were pumping the water from the Gulf on one side of the boat to the other. He wondered why they had not yet sunk, given how much water had gotten into the bilge. The captain staggered forward until he made his way inside. The sky darkened further, suggesting that night had fallen, yet the storm continued to rage while the *White Whale* fought to find land.

CHAPTER FIFTEEN

Jim dragged the boat by its anchor chain. It had already grounded, but it would be safer farther up the shore. He clenched his teeth and dug his soaked boots into the sand as he pulled. Step by agonizing step, the boat crunched and ground its way forward until the prow hung over the soft sand above the high-tide line.

He fell back to sit in the sand while rain poured down, exhausted. Even his great strength was spent, but the lightning was far out at sea, leaving the land alone to suffer under a gully-washer. Once he dropped his head between his knees, he could not lift it again. Wolfe concentrated his efforts on the simple task of breathing.

Wolfe had left Rusty and the captain on board. A wave had swamped them when they were coming through the breakers, flooding the boiler and killing the flame. The last few seconds of steam kept the propeller turning long enough to deliver the boat into knee-deep water. That was when the captain and Rusty collapsed.

That was when Wolfe took over.

After his heart slowed, Wolfe struggled to stand, walking

inland to a house on the beach to find shelter on its porch. He did not consider whether anyone lived there or not. The cushions on the swinging chair should have told him that people were there, but he was too tired to do anything except sleep.

He awoke to someone poking him. He pulled his goggles up. They were coated with salt and sand. He did not dare wipe them off. He needed to rinse them under clean water.

"My name is Jim Wolfe, and we beached down below. The storm caught us off-guard," he explained, unable to see who he was talking to.

"Mom!" a young voice shouted before footsteps pounded away.

Wolfe pinched his eyes closed and took off his goggles, shaking them to get rid of the sand. The drip of water falling into water drew his eye. A barrel was collecting rainwater from the downspout. Wolfe dipped his goggles in and shook them out. When he put them back on, he found a middle-aged woman glaring at him.

"We drink that," she declared, fists wedged into her hips.

"My apologies, ma'am. My eyes are sensitive to light, and I need these to see in the daytime. I will make this right if you just tell me what I need to do."

She huffed and sighed. "Take your boat off our beach and be on your way."

"I think it will take a bit of work to get the boat running again. May I ask where we are?"

"This place is called Horseshoe Beach."

"How far to Tampa Bay from here?"

"You have to go east from here to catch a road south through Suwannee and then keep going south. It is about a hundred twenty miles, but there is no reason to go. There is nothing left."

"I have heard that, ma'am. My family was in Bradenton

when the bombs fell. It has taken me this long to get this close. I need to see it for myself."

"I understand, mister, but do not come back here if you go there. You'll be covered in radiation and dying," the woman replied. "And you still need to get your boat off my beach."

"We will. I will go check on them now and see if we can get an estimate of how long it will be. We have some bluefin tuna we can provide to you to offset the inconvenience."

The woman licked her lips. A girl maybe five years old hid behind her, hanging onto the back of the woman's pants.

"Let me know," the woman conceded before shooing her daughter into the house.

Wolfe left the house and returned to the beach. Sunrise had brought the makings of a beautiful day. A cloudless sky smiled down on him. A faint breeze blew in off the ocean. The *White Whale* looked abandoned as it perched awkwardly on the sand, the barnacles on its hull covered with seaweed and still dripping saltwater.

He climbed aboard over the lowest railing, looking for the captain and Rusty. Navigating the slanting deck was a challenge, but he made it below into the small cabin where he found the two men, still asleep, both in the same rack, wedged into the corner between the mattress and bulkhead. When he checked their pulses, he found they were fine.

The captain forced his eyes open. "We are alive," he croaked. He tried to move but could not. He saw the reason. "Get off me."

Wolfe helped pull Rusty away. The young man never woke up. Wolfe deposited him back into the rack after the captain was upright.

"This place is called Horseshoe Beach, a little over a hundred miles north of Tampa."

"How is my boat?" the captain asked, looking around. The

aft end of the cabin had standing water that should not have been there. Wolfe went topside, found his pack, and checked to make sure it had his stuff.

"I will run the bilge pump to empty the water, but then I am going to take the land route to Bradenton. I will be back as soon as I can."

"You are leaving?" the captain muttered in disbelief.

"I am so close. I *have to know*. I can make it there in a couple of days. Please wait for me, but if you cannot, then go ahead. I will get back to Mobile on foot. Tell Miss Jennifer that I am coming for her."

The captain pulled himself along to get out of the cabin and onto the deck. Wolfe danced to the bilge pump and started cranking. Bilge water poured onto the sand. He kept working the pump as the captain talked.

"I cannot guarantee the *White Whale* will ever go back into the water." The captain ran his fingers through a greasy shock of black hair. He frowned at the thought. "But we will do our best."

Wolfe chuckled. "You may have to deal with the owner of the house up the beach. She seemed none too pleased about a boat on her beach."

"Bah!" The captain shook his head. "At least before the bombs, no one, not even the richest, could have a private beach. All ocean and Gulf beaches were guaranteed public access. I do not want to fight with her, but getting the *Whale* seaworthy is going to take a lot of work."

The stream of foul water coming from the bilge lessened. When it became a trickle, Wolfe locked up the pump and went for his backpack and rifle.

"You might want to hit that with a little oil," the captain told him. The rust was already starting.

"Much obliged," Wolfe replied. The captain dug into a

drawer beside the steering column and removed a small bottle.

"For your gun. I have more. We'll have to clean out the boiler and oil everything afresh. We probably have two weeks' worth of work before we think about how to get the boat off this beach, assuming we do not find anything that we cannot fix."

The captain leaned back, bloodshot eyes staring into the welding goggles as if he could see into Wolfe's soul. Wolfe offered his hand.

The man hesitated before taking it. "You are going?"

"Have to," Wolfe answered simply. "Just like I have to come back. My word, Ahab."

"I look forward to seeing you again, Jim. You are one of the good ones."

Wolfe nodded, tight-lipped. Without another word, he climbed off the ship and headed inland toward the morning sun until he reached a highway heading south. He was in familiar territory. It was different, but he had been there before. Wolfe hitched his pack onto his shoulders, checked how it rode, and started jogging.

CHAPTER SIXTEEN

W hen Wolfe reached Otter Creek less than an hour later, he was still wet from where he had to ford a stream. A bridge had fallen, but it looked like it had been dropped using dynamite. Someone had intentionally cut off the small peninsula from the rest of Florida.

Wolfe stopped into the small town at a crossroads where the county road met a highway. Highway 98 led straight to Tampa. Back in the day, it had too many speed zones and stops to make it worthwhile. It was easier and quicker to travel a longer route by taking the interstate farther inland. Wolfe wanted the shortest route because he was on foot.

He broke down his rifle while carefully drinking from his canteen. There was a creek in town, but the water looked foul. Wolfe did not know if that was the real Otter Creek or not. He would continue south. There were more streams and rivers not far away. Many had flowed well at one time. He expected their water would be clean enough to drink. He needed it to be since he did not want to waste time boiling it.

At least, that was what he hoped. His plan did not include much at this point besides finishing his run home. He broke down the cleaned and oiled rifle and stuffed it into his backpack, then tied off his canteen and started running again. Wolfe picked up the pace until it was almost a sprint. He had more energy than usual because the end was in sight.

Five miles became ten became twenty. After three hours of sprinting, Wolfe was halfway to his goal. What he did not see were any signs of life. He had felt slight tingles as he ran, but nothing hot enough to hold him back. The vegetation was growing well, the heat and humidity bringing it to a Florida level of bushiness. So much water and sun. The plants fed well.

Where were the humans? Birds flew overhead. Seagulls. An egret passed to the south.

If the birds could thrive, so could man. Maybe they had not returned because the Tampa area had been termed a wasteland, and that message had been perpetuated across the land.

He had heard it as far away as Arkansas.

But there were people in Horseshoe Beach. Not many, from what he saw, but enough that they had themselves a community. Maybe that was as far south as anyone went. He did not see them using electricity or hear any machines running. It had become a simple coastal community, probably counting on fishing for subsistence. Some light farming, too.

Wolfe walked quickly instead of sitting. He considered himself to be resting, but he could not stop. He figured he would run to the outskirts, increasing his pace with the darkness when he could remove his goggles and enjoy the relative cool of the night. The heat and the humidity did not bother him, not as much as it could have. He emptied his canteen and started running again at a steady ten miles per hour.

It was not long before he arrived at Crystal Springs. Signs

for Tampa appeared along the road. Restaurants. Stores. Lawyers. Wolfe stopped to orient himself. With the unrestricted regrowth, even the most urban of areas were being reclaimed by nature. Once he figured out where he was, he walked east, looking for a small lake with a park. It had had clear water in the before time. He expected that it would have remained unmolested.

It turned out to be better than he'd remembered. Wolfe checked the area for gators, but the water was shallow and clear. He did not see where anything could hide. The first thing he did was rinse his goggles again, vigorously shaking them dry to keep them as scratch-free as possible for as long as he could. He thought for a moment before stripping down and climbing in. With a precious bar of soap that Jennifer had insisted he carry, he scrubbed himself clean, then washed out his clothes and hung them across branches to dry. The heat had grown oppressive, and he knew he needed to wait until later when it started to cool to continue his journey.

Plus, the darkness was his friend.

He had a bad feeling about the area, and it was getting worse. The only other times he had seen areas that were clean of radiation but abandoned were when the wilders or Central Command had been in charge, keeping the people afraid.

Wolfe drank deeply of the fresh water. The wound across his chest was mostly healed, but he had not yet bothered to remove the stitches. He took his knife and sharpened the blade with a few strokes across the sharpening stone he carried.

He cut himself in the attempt but removed two more stitches before he gave up. He would have to do it in the darkness when the goggles weren't in the way unless he could find a mirror. Naked as the day he was born, carrying his rifle and backpack, he saw the small bathroom in the park. Oddly, it was locked, but Wolfe ripped the rusting hasp out of the metal door jamb. He opened the door and walked inside. The heat was oppressive, but it did not smell like a park's toilet normally would, not that he would have cared if it had.

When he shut the door, it was dark inside, dark enough that he risked pulling his goggles off one eye. It was bright, but not so bad that he had to put the goggles back on. He went to work on his chest. Between the mirror and being able to see directly, he removed the stitches with the minimum amount of grief. Miss Jennifer would have done a better job.

Why did you make her stay behind? Wolfe asked himself. He knew the answer. He did not want her to see him crushed when he learned the truth. He left the bathroom and strolled across the open area, still self-conscious, even though he was the only one there. His eyes darted around the area, looking for movement. He put his wet clothes back on, choosing to let them dry on his body. He stretched as he walked, preparing himself to run sixty miles that night if he could.

He dug out the last of the smoked bear he had carried into Mobile. They had had access to plenty of other food without digging into their emergency stocks. Now was the time. He would worry about eating after he had seen what he came to see.

Still wet, he threw on his pack, took one last look for the eyes he could feel were watching him, and returned to the main road. He started running again, setting a pace no normal human could match. Wolfe knew exactly where he was and which way to go.

He turned onto a toll road, sprinting through the extended suburbs of Tampa. In two hours, he covered thirty miles, but then he needed to slow down. The nagging feeling was too much. He moved off the road to stay in the shadows.

Darkness had not yet fallen, but the sun was low in the sky. Wolfe tested exposed surfaces but could not feel the tingle of radiation. That gave him hope.

The first hint that he was not alone was the noise. He heard yelling and shouting, as if people who were hard of hearing were having a party.

He slowed further. Moving from building to building in a crouch, he looked for a vantage point and spotted a three-story building with a flat roof. He worked his way inside and climbed the stairs, breaking through two doors before he found the roof access—a ladder to an overhead cover. He pushed his way outside, blinking behind his goggles as the evening sun shone directly into his face. He turned away, staying low until he reached the retaining wall. He peeked over, turning his head to find the source of the noise.

Two blocks away, partially hidden by a smaller building, there was a checkpoint. He had seen the likes of those manning it before.

Wilders. And they had caught a group of unsuspecting travelers.

CHAPTER SEVENTEEN

Wolfe's blood boiled. He could see two women, naked and tied to a telephone pole. Two men lay at their feet in what Wolfe suspected were puddles of their own blood. The women screamed intermittently as the wilders danced around them, drinking and touching their prey.

That was enough for him. "Lurleen, forgive me," he begged, knowing that she would have told him to save the victims.

He raced down the ladder and the steps, heading out the back door and along a street that paralleled the one on which the wilders had set up their checkpoint. He leaned around the corner of the building. Only three wilders.

Maybe that was why the two couples had approached them. They had thought it was four against three, but it had been no contest. Wilders did not think like normal people. They did not act like them, either. Wolfe growled low in his throat, then removed his rifle and quickly put it together. He clicked a full magazine home and put two others in his pockets. He carried his backpack as he climbed through a window of the building he had been hiding behind.

He worked his way to the front. A display window was shattered, the dummies destroyed and rotting. He set his pack down and crawled forward, slipping the barrel of the gun over the last dummy, keeping the barrel back from the windowsill to prevent the wilders from seeing it. He watched as they danced.

He needed the three to move away from the women, but they were close. Too close. But Wolfe was close, too. They were only thirty yards away. He could cover that in a matter of seconds. Two men carried knives, the other, only a bottle.

Wolfe bunched his legs beneath him, adjusted his grip on the rifle, and jumped through the window, running at the men as fast as he could.

They did not notice him for a second, but then one stopped and pointed stupidly. Wolfe did not try to shoot while running. He was afraid of hitting the women. With a shout, he was on them.

The first went down when the butt of the rifle slammed into his face. Wolfe jumped and twisted, slashing the barrel down on the man closest to the captives. The last man brandished his knife and squared off. Wolfe aimed from his waist and fired. The round hit the man in the chest, tumbling after it hit his breastbone, sending shards of the split metal jacket through the man's insides. He was thrown backward, dead before he hit the ground.

The first wilder was struggling to get to his feet. Wolfe aimed and fired, and the man dropped into a growing pool of his own blood. The dent in the skull of the third suggested he was every bit as dead as the other two.

Wolfe looked around for reinforcements. With his ears still ringing from the gunfire, he could not hear if anyone was coming.

He picked up the dropped knife and cut the women free. They both went to the two men who had been on the ground, men Wolfe assumed had been with them. A groan told him they were not dead.

Wolfe moved to the checkpoint, where the women's clothes were draped like flags on the refuse blocking the street. He recovered them and hurried back to the two, giving them their clothes before heading into the building to get his backpack. He did not know if he would have to run anytime soon.

He gave the women time to get dressed before returning.

They had both men sitting up against a small shop. Wolfe was happy to see they were alive.

"Thank you, mister," one of the women said, not looking up or meeting Wolfe's eyes.

"Do you know if there are more men like these around here?" Wolfe asked.

They shook their heads. "We came from the north, escaped the camp."

"The camp?" Wolfe wondered. He kneeled to be eye-level with the four refugees.

"Where everyone went after the bombs fell, or at least those who were able to get out."

The second woman had not spoken. She ministered to the second man as if there was nothing else going on in the world.

"Where are you from?" Wolfe's mind started to spin.

"Bradenton," the woman replied.

"I am from Bradenton," he blurted before catching himself. "When were you last there?"

"Four years ago. We were coming home from Disney-world when it happened. Mushroom clouds over Tampa Bay and behind us in Orlando. We headed north but never made it out of Florida. They were corralling refugees in Jacksonville. Then a war broke out between the people and the People's Government. Everyone who survived ended up in the camps. We were in the worst of them. It was called Andersonville after the Civil War camp."

"Do you know a Lurleen Wolfe? She would have been with a little fella, my JoJo."

"I'm sorry, mister. I do not." She turned to the others. The woman shook her head slightly, showing she had been listening. One of the men also shook his head, even though he had not yet opened his eyes."

Wolfe stood and listened. Silence had returned.

"I need to climb up there and take a look," Wolfe said. "Make sure no more wilders are about."

"Wilders?"

"They live in the hot zone. They do not abide by the law or common decency." Wolfe nodded once and jogged away. A short antenna tower was nearby, but it was taller than all the buildings in the area. Wolfe slung his pack and rifle on his back and started to climb. He hurried upward, stopping every ten to fifteen feet to look. Wilders had to come from somewhere, but then again, he was jaded by Central Command. They were organized. This bunch was not.

He was not sorry they were dead. Wolfe thought he should have felt something, but he did not. Reclaiming the world for the good people had become his mission. He did not want to be the one to deliver justice from the end of his rifle, but that was what it had come to. The innocent could not protect themselves from the savages.

But Wolfe could protect them.

He climbed to forty feet and stopped, bracing himself as he watched for movement. Tampa was too far away to see. He chewed on the inside of his cheek as he waited, watching the checkpoint, too. The refugees stayed where they were, not trying to get away. At one point, the quiet woman walked to one of the dead men and started kicking him in the head.

The other woman grabbed her by the shoulders and sat her down with the other two in their party.

That was the world Wolfe's family had been left to.

"I am sorry, Lurleen, sorry I was not there for you." She did not answer. She would not blame anyone. She did not judge him because she knew that being gone from home to earn money for the family was just as hard on him as it was on her. She would have never let him say he was sorry for doing what had to be done.

Like killing the three wilders. He was not the man to revel in sitting in judgment of others, but those men were criminals, in this world and in the next. They would pay for their crimes in the afterlife. Wolfe was convinced of it. He wondered what his fate was. Probably the same. He had killed a great number of people since the bombs fell.

A great number. He had lost track long ago.

No one was coming. Wolfe climbed back down and returned to the two couples. They were surprised to see him, recoiling at the sight of his rifle as if it were a new threat.

"I will be on my way. I only wanted to be sure you were safe before I went. There is a community at Horseshoe Beach, about a hundred miles up the road. Follow Highway 98 until you can take a left on SW-351. You will have to walk through a creek, but that is so no one can easily get there. They are staying away from the rest of humanity. It might be a good place to live in peace."

The first man had recovered sufficiently to stand, although he hobbled and held his chest as if he had broken ribs.

"Thank you, mister. It would be easier if we had some way to protect ourselves." His eyes glanced to the bow tied to the pack and then the rifle in Wolfe's arms."

"I expect you will be able to find something along the

way," Wolfe replied. "I am going that way, into the heart of it. If there are more like those three, I will deal with them."

"We figured there would not be anyone down here. They surprised us. We had seen no one until we got here. Maybe you can come with us. You are going to find that there's nothing left and probably get yourself fried by the radiation in the process." The young woman spoke more confidently since she felt safer.

"You need to get yourselves away from here in case these three had friends." Wolfe did not want to spend more time with banter. He had a ways to go, and the sun had set. "I have to go. Good luck."

He walked away, shortly breaking into a run to return to the main toll road and keep going south toward Tampa Bay.

CHAPTER EIGHTEEN

The destruction was clear. The fires had burned out long ago. Buildings had toppled well outside the initial blast. Wolfe had to turn east two miles from the downtown to swing wide around the worst of it. Radiation lingered. He avoided touching anything and ran quickly, lifting his feet to kick up as little dust as possible until he was well clear. He ran all the way to Interstate 75 to get around the bay and to the south side, where Bradenton was located.

When he was due east of Tampa Bay, the destruction was apparent and complete. The area was so hot it continued to glow. Wolfe gritted his teeth and ran on. He had twenty miles to go, and the way ahead looked clear. Dawn was a few hours away. Wolfe ran with his goggles around his neck. He could see better that way, so he increased speed. He breathed harder with his efforts, but each stride brought him closer to Bradenton and took him farther from the destruction that was Tampa Bay.

Two hours later, he found himself jogging since he could not maintain the torrid pace any longer. He was a mile from home, and Bradenton looked abandoned. It also looked looted.

Which meant that it had survived the blast and most of the initial radiation. He reached toward buildings, vehicles, and puddles but could not feel any tingling. He breathed a sigh of relief and started running again, his legs protesting the effort.

He turned on a road he had driven a thousand times before and then onto his home street. Most of the front doors were missing, including his. He raced inside, yelling Lurleen's name. There was no answer. He had not expected one.

No one had been there for years. Maybe since weeks after the bombs fell. JoJo's bedroom was intact, with his little bed still covered by the blanket with a spaceship.

His and Lurleen's bedroom was messy, as if she had raced around pulling the suitcases from the closet and filling them with random things.

The jewelry cases on the dresser had been dumped and the nicer pieces taken. Wolfe did not care about any of that. He had seen the value of jewelry over the past four years. It was worthless compared to a rifle and ammunition or a bow and good arrows.

Wolfe was hungry and sore. He was exhausted in all ways and finding it hard to stand up straight, yet he worked his way through his home, looking through each room. In the kitchen, most of the food was gone, and the rest was spoiled. He found a lone can of baked beans behind a bag of moldy rice. He opened it with a military can opener he kept in his pack and inhaled the contents while sitting at his table on the chair that he had claimed as his. These beans had been his favorite of the canned. Lurleen made better. She used to sit right there.

He hung his head. Broken dishes and decorations from the counters littered the tile floor.

Along with a paper with Lurleen's handwriting.

Jim. I hope you get this. JoJo and I were told to evacuate. None of the cars work so we had to walk. He is strong, and we will be fine. We are supposed to be going to Jacksonville. Please join us there as soon as you can. I love you with all my heart. L.

Jacksonville. A civil war. Andersonville.

Wolfe carefully folded the paper and tucked it into his pocket. He returned to his bedroom, closing and locking the door behind him. He crawled on top of the musty covers. In the evening, when the sun started to set, he was leaving for Jacksonville to find his wife and son.

The End
Nightwalker Book 7

Wolfe will return in *Nightwalker* 8, the thrilling conclusion to Frank Roderus' *Nightwalker* series. Follow the series here - https://geni.us/Nightwalker

If you like this book, please leave a review. Your opinion matters to me. I will write book 8, but when? If we get enough reviews, it will be sooner rather than later. I have only so much time to craft new stories. Help me invest that time wisely. Plus, reviews buoy my spirits and stoke the fires of creativity.

Don't stop now! There's more...

AUTHOR NOTES - CRAIG MARTELLE

WRITTEN MARCH 24, 2020

You are still reading! Thank you for continuing all the way.

It's the start of the COVID-19 lockdown. I finished this book a month ago, well before the changes in how we live our lives. Here's a secret. Not much has changed for me. My life was mostly a quarantine. I always cleaned the handle of my shopping cart with the wipes at the entrance of the store. Once I started doing that, I got sick a lot less. And that was the only thing I was doing differently. Now, we are being far more diligent. That's okay. Can't let the virus break into our personal castles:)

It's more a battle of personal discipline than anything else (unless you're a truck driver or medical professional and then you're fighting a different battle). The rest of us just have to practice medical-grade hygiene. It's not something we're used to, but the longer it takes for us to figure it out, the worse we will unintentionally make things.

And then we get back to the everyday. For us, it's the spring thaw which we call break up in Alaska. Because over the winter, we develop a hard pack of snow from what we've driven on (and packed down) or what we've walked on. Six months' worth of snow usually takes a while to melt. The way it works up here is that October snow finally melts in April. When temps dip below freezing in the fall, they stay there until the sun is hitting us for longer than twelve hours a day, which starts in later March.

I tell people that we have six months of winter. I'm not kidding. We had a big snowstorm the past few days and there is more coming. But temps are warm. It's two in the morning right now and thirty-three degrees. The most recent snowfall is already starting to clear itself. I cleaned off my truck last night. The final tidbits from the sweeping have melted away.

I know what you're thinking. But you love your truck? Why would you park it outside when you have that lovely garage? Let me tell you. My wife was in Spain at the worst of the pandemic's beginning. She was able to catch one of the last series of flights that got her home, but she's now in mandatory quarantine in the house, and I'm in a hotel in town. My poor truck is outside and has been for nine days now. But it is plugged in to keep the engine warm. I take it on little drives just to get out of the hotel room.

I am getting a lot done, though. Eyes are starting to go buggy from looking at a computer screen for too long, but I'm over halfway finished with Judge, Jury, & Executioner 9. I'm back to my old writing speed and then some. So, there is that.

I hope you enjoyed Nightwalker 7. Nightwalker 8 will wrap up this series and that will be coming in just a few months. Thank you all for staying on board with Frank Roderus' series. I hope that I'm doing it justice.

Peace, fellow humans.

Please join my Newsletter (craigmartelle.com—please,

please, please sign up!), or you can follow me on Facebook since you'll get the same opportunity to pick up books for only 99 cents when they go on sale.

If you liked this story, you might like some of my other books. You can join my mailing list by dropping by my website at craigmartelle.com, or if you have any comments, shoot me a note at craig@craigmartelle.com. I am always happy to hear from people who've read my work. I try to answer every email I receive.

If you liked the story, please write a short review for me on Amazon. I greatly appreciate any kind words, and even one or two sentences go a long way. The number of reviews an ebook receives greatly improves how well it does on Amazon.

Amazon – www.amazon.com/author/craigmartelle

BookBub – https://www.bookbub.com/authors/craig-martelle

Facebook – www.facebook.com/authorcraigmartelle

My web page – www.craigmartelle.com

That's it—break's over, back to writing the next book.

ABOUT THE AUTHOR

Frank Roderus wrote his first story—it was a western—when he was five. It was really awful, as might be expected, but his mother kept that typed and spell-checked short story tucked away until the day she died.

Later, Frank became a newspaper reporter, thinking that books are written by authors which he most assuredly was not. He kept trying to write though, and eventually did it wrong enough to learn how to get it right. That first sale, a young adult novel published by Independence Press, was more than thirty years and a good many books ago.

As a journalist, the Colorado Press Association awarded Frank Roderus their highest award, the Sweepstakes Award, for the best news story of 1980, and the Western Writers of America has twice named Frank recipient of their prestigious Spur Award.

Frank passed away at age 73 in December 2015.

BOOKS BY CRAIG MARTELLE

Craig Martelle's other books (listed by series)

Terry Henry Walton Chronicles (co-written with Michael Anderle) – a post-apocalyptic paranormal adventure

Gateway to the Universe (co-written with Justin Sloan & Michael Anderle) – this book transitions the characters from the Terry Henry Walton Chronicles to The Bad Company

The Bad Company (co-written with Michael Anderle) – a military science fiction space opera

Judge, Jury, & Executioner (also available in audio) – a space opera adventure legal thriller

Shadow Vanguard – a Tom Dublin series

Superdreadnought (co-written with Tim Marquitz)– an AI military space opera

Metal Legion (co-written with Caleb Wachter) (coming in audio) – a military space opera

The Free Trader – a young adult science fiction action-adventure

Cygnus Space Opera (also available in audio) – A young adult space opera (set in the Free Trader universe)

Darklanding (co-written with Scott Moon) (also available in audio) – a space western

Mystically Engineered (co-written with Valerie Emerson) – Mystics, dragons, & spaceships

End Times Alaska (also available in audio) – a Permuted Press publication – a post-apocalyptic survivalist adventure

Nightwalker (a Frank Roderus series) with Craig Martelle – A post-apocalyptic western adventure

End Days (co-written with E.E. Isherwood) (coming in audio) – a post-apocalyptic adventure

Successful Indie Author – a non-fiction series to help self-published authors

Metamorphosis Alpha – stories from the world's first science fiction RPG

The Expanding Universe – science fiction anthologies

Monster Case Files (co-written with Kathryn Hearst) – A Warner twins mystery adventure

Rick Banik (also available in audio) – Spy & terrorism action adventure

Published exclusively by Craig Martelle, Inc

The Dragon's Call by Angelique Anderson & Craig A. Price, Jr. – an epic fantasy quest

For a complete list of Craig's books, stop by his website – https://craigmartelle.com